then came
HOPE

BUFFY ANDREWS

Andrews Creative Concepts
York, Pennsylvania 17404
andrewscreativeconcepts.com

Print ISBN: 978-1-7374351-7-4
Ebook ISBN: 978-1-7374351-8-1

Published in the United States of America

To my dearest sons, Zach and Micah

I have watched in awe as you have grown into incredible young men, each with your own unique spirit and dreams. You've faced challenges with resilience, pursued your passions with unwavering determination and embraced life with a zest that inspires me beyond measure.

Remember, my sons, that you possess the strength to overcome any obstacle, the courage to chase your dreams and the compassion to make a positive impact on the world.

All my love, Mom

Prologue

Seasons come and seasons go, and more and more headstones sprout from the once fertile farmland on the edge of town. I walk through this cemetery, remembering the white, wooden church that once stood sentinel at the turn of the century. Torn down long ago, the only hint of its existence is a set of stone steps that lead nowhere.

A row of thick forsythia, the color of marigolds, waves in the spring breeze. The smell of freshly cut grass tickles my nose. The warmth of the sun makes me long for lazy days spent reading under the apple tree in my backyard.

It is here where I spend my time, never knowing who I might see. I've met a lot of folks while on my daily strolls, most weighed down by a boulder of grief too heavy to carry. That is why I walk. Maybe, just maybe, I can lift the boulder and make it a bit lighter.

Tavi

I always believed things happened for a reason. I don't anymore. What reason could there possibly be for losing the two most important people in my life? I should've been in the car with Tom and Aiden, but I wasn't. Instead, I was wrapped in a blanket cocoon, recovering from a nasty bug that had swept through the office.

Life is cruel with its twists and turns, and just when you think you've found happiness, it can be seized in seconds without warning or apology.

Police said the teenager ran the stop sign. One night, one second, one mistake, and three lives lost.

For the past two days, I've felt as if I were watching a drama of someone else's life, a bittersweet film montage dissolving into darkness. I constantly hit the rewind button, needing desperately to return to a time when life was sweeter and thick with promises of great tomorrows.

I stared at the digital pregnancy test I'd picked up at the drugstore on the way home. I'd had a miscarriage the year before, after years of trying, and I was desperate to be pregnant again.

While a part of me was terrified at what might happen if I became pregnant, another part of me didn't want to give up trying. I wanted... No, I *needed* to know that I had the ability to do this—to carry to term a beautiful baby that Tom and I had created.

I knew that if I was ever lucky enough to become pregnant again, I'd be filled with a lot of fear and anxiety, especially at first. But not trying was worse.

My eyes were glued to the pregnancy test screen, praying for a second chance to be a mommy. An hourglass flashed as the test was processed and then...

Omigosh! Omigosh! Omigosh! I'm pregnant!

I look into the mirror. My face looks like a bloated beet. A tear breaks loose and slides down my splotchy cheek. I taste salt on my lower lip, and reach for a tissue, dabbing the snail-like trace on my cheek left by the renegade tear. I shouldn't have bothered. A torrent of tears follows, and I cry myself to sleep once more.

"Tavi, it's time to get up."

I hear Kacie's voice and feel her tug at my arm. My eyelids hang heavy like brocade stage curtains. I want to remain in the darkness. Opening my eyes means going back to a reality I'm not sure I'm strong enough to face. I want to tell her to go away and to leave me alone. I don't care about living anymore. I want to be with Tom and Aiden.

"Tav, it's time to get ready."

I crack my eyes. I need Kacie more than I've ever needed her. I have to get through Tom and Aiden's viewing and funeral. Mom will be there, too, but she's never shown me much compassion. If truth be told, I'm not sure she ever loved me. I was Daddy's little girl and grew up feeling her resentment. *Go ahead. Run to your father. Of course, he'll side with you. He always does.*

When Dad died of a massive heart attack in his mid-fifties, she blamed me. *He was always worrying about you. Tavi this and Tavi that.* I remember how he'd come home after work and scoop me up in his arms and twirl me around as if we were the only two people in the world who mattered. I'd laugh, and when he put me down, I'd beg for him to do it again and again.

After Dad died, Mom and I didn't have much to talk about. We'd go weeks without speaking, and I was the one who usually ended up calling out of guilt. I'm not sure how the chasm between us grew so wide, but I'll count on Kacie to keep her at bay.

Mom and I stood next to Dad's bronze casket and greeted those who came to pay their last respects. A tall guy dressed in a black suit, white shirt and red tie approached. He didn't look much older than me.

"I'm Tom Jackson." He shook Mom's hand. "Henry was a great mentor and a great person. I'll never forget all he did for me."

Mom smiled. "Thank you. You're the young man who joined the hospital last summer."

Tom nodded.

"Henry spoke highly of you. Thank you for coming."

Tom looked at me, his sad brown eyes boring into mine. "And you must be Tavi."

I managed to smile. "Yes."

"You have your dad's smile. He never stopped talking about you."

I dabbed my eyes with the tissue I clutched in my hand. "Thanks. I couldn't have asked for a better father."

I manage to crawl out of bed and ease into the shower, thankful that Kacie had spent the night. She and her husband, Jack, are expecting their first child, and Kacie is just beginning to show. A small mound protrudes from her normally flat stomach.

We'd always dreamed that our kids would grow up together. Aiden would have been four by the time Kacie had her baby. I picture Aiden cradling a newborn as Kacie and I snap photos. Then I picture the two coffins I picked out placed side by side in the dark, cold earth.

Stop it, Tavi. Stop it! My heart starts to race, and I feel as if the shower walls are caving in on me. *Deep breaths! Deep breaths!* I quickly rinse my hair and pop open the shower door.

Whew! Whew!

I dry off and realize I forgot to shave my legs. *Who cares? It's not like anyone is going to feel them.* I wrap the pink towel around my head, making it look like the top of a strawberry ice-cream cone. I smile ever so slightly, torn between a sweet memory of Tom and I sharing an ice-cream cone on our first date and the reality that I will never share another one with him—ever!

There's a knock on my bedroom door. "Tav, do you need any help?"

"No, Kacie. I'm fine. Is Mom here?"

"She just called to say she's running a little late and will meet us at the funeral home."

I'm not surprised. For most of my life, Mom has never been on time for anything—my fourth-grade talent show, high school awards ceremony and college graduation among them. And I'm sure that if it hadn't been for Kacie, she would've been late to my wedding.

I'm still not sure how Kacie managed to get Mom there on time, but I always figured Mom did it for Kacie more than she did it for me. Growing up, whenever Kacie was around, Mom would compliment her constantly. Kacie always tried to shift the attention to me, but Mom never seemed to care. I always felt that she would've liked to have had Kacie as a daughter instead of me.

I sit on the edge of my bed and pick up my pantyhose. I roll up the left leg, thinking how much I hate wearing them. They're tight, they itch and they're a hassle getting on and off. But then I realize how stupid these thoughts are. *Pantyhose. Really, Tavi? You're complaining about how uncomfortable pantyhose are? Your husband and son are dead!*

I stand and pick up the black dress I laid on the bed earlier. I own two black dresses, and I didn't think either was appropriate. The first I bought when Tom and I went to a New Year's Eve party. It was short and sexy and clung to my curvy five-foot six-inch frame. The second was long with a sequined, tight bodice and looked way too formal for a funeral. Thankfully, Kacie loaned me her long-sleeved, matte jersey wrap, and it is perfect.

I walk into the kitchen, where Kacie is sipping a cup of tea and checking her email on her cell phone. She looks up at me. "You look great."

My eyes begin to water, and I'm thankful that I used waterproof mascara.

Kacie stands. "I'm sorry. That was probably a stupid thing to say." She hugs me, and I hug her back, and for a few seconds we embrace in silence. I know that Kacie and everyone else mean well, but looking good is the last thing I care about.

Kacie pulls back from the hug and looks me in the eye. "I will help you get through this."

I nod, knowing that Kacie has always had my back.

Kacie jumped between me and Tina Marshall, my high school nemesis.

"Back off!" Kacie snarled. "Tavi had nothing to do with Ben dumping you."

I watched as Kacie stared down at Tina. I'd always admired Kacie's grit. Maybe it was the byproduct of having four older brothers who taught her not to take crap from anyone. Kacie was the toughest and strongest girl I knew.

Tina looked past Kacie at me. "Stay out of my way."

"No," Kacie threatened, jabbing her index finger into Tina's chest. "You stay out of *our* way."

"I made a fresh pot of coffee," Kacie says. "You should try to eat a little something."

I open the kitchen cabinet to get a coffee mug and see a photo of Aiden. I pick up the photo mug Tom had given me on my first Mother's Day. Aiden is dressed in jeans and a red polo shirt, size three months.

I breathe in deeply, trying to keep the tears at bay. I feel Kacie's eyes on me. I pick up another mug, one with no special meaning, and fill it with coffee.

"How about some eggs?" Kacie asks.

"I know I should eat something," I tell Kacie. "But I have no appetite."

"Maybe some toast?"

I nod. "I'll try."

I manage to eat most of the toast and down another cup of coffee, along with the pills the doctor had given me to settle my nerves. I touch my diamond engagement ring and wedding band, cuddling together on my ring finger. I sniff, remembering as clearly as ice the day Tom proposed to me.

"How did you manage to get a long weekend off?" I asked Tom.

"Pete likes you, and I told him I wanted to take you to the beach for your birthday."

"You mean it?"

Tom nodded. "Yep, I have everything booked."

A week later, we stood on the beach, digging our toes into the sugary white sand.

"I don't know of anything that's more beautiful," I said.

"I do," said Tom, pausing until I looked at him. "You."

He reached inside his pocket and knelt on the sand. "Tavi Peters. Will you marry me?"

My hands covered my heart, and I gasped. Tears stained my cheeks. My lips trembled, and I couldn't speak. I nodded and melted into his arms, feeling more loved than I ever had.

Kacie and I walk into the funeral home. It seems odd to have Tom and Aiden's service here instead of in a church, but it's what Tom wanted. It's what he was used to and what his family always did. Mine, on the other hand, would never think of having a funeral service in any place but the family church.

Generations of Peters had attended the Lutheran church in the small, southcentral Pennsylvania town where we lived. Scratches made by my great-great-grandfather's suspenders etch the pew where we sat—right side, third row from the back.

I stop right inside the entrance to look at the photo collage Kacie put together, and I lose my footing. She reaches for me and props me up. "I got you, Tav."

Tears stream down my cheeks as I scan the photos. Me holding a newborn Aiden in the hospital. Aiden sitting in a highchair with cake and icing all over his hands and face from digging into his first birthday cake. Tom mowing the lawn, and Aiden following behind pushing the toy mower Mom bought him for his second birthday. Aiden wearing a chef's hat and helping me bake Christmas cookies. The ends of my mouth curl as I notice more red and green sprinkles on him than on the cookies.

I turn and bury my head on Kacie's shoulder. She rubs my back. "I'm not sure I can do this," I say.

"I can't begin to imagine how you feel," Kacie whispers. "But I hope you know that I'm here, and that you're not alone."

I stand and take one last look at the display. My eyes fixate on a photo of me and Tom taken on our wedding day. We look so young. And happy. It seems like a lifetime ago.

My heart beat so fast that it felt like it was going to pop out of my chest. I looked up at Daddy, and his eyes glistened. "You're the most beautiful bride I've ever seen," he said.

As we walked down the aisle, I was glad I was getting married in our church. I hadn't wanted to at first. I wanted an outdoor wedding at the country club where the reception was being held. But a church wedding seemed to mean so much to Dad, and the last thing I wanted to do was disappoint him.

"Who presents this woman to be married to this man?" the minister asked.

"Her mother and I do," Dad said.

Kacie leads me into the large gathering room, and we walk up to the coffins. I notice the teddy bear Tom bought Aiden after he was born nestled next to my baby boy. Aiden, wearing a small black suit that matches Tom's, looks like a little man. *A little man who will never grow up, never marry, or have children of his own.*

My chin wobbles, and my knees buckle. I grasp the side of Tom's coffin, trying to steady myself. The room begins to spin in a tornado blur. I'm lightheaded and nauseous. *Don't vomit, Tavi. Don't vomit!*

I let go of the coffin and fell to the floor, burying my head in my open hands. It's just too much. My chest hurts, and my heart pounds out of control. I can't catch my breath.

Omigosh! I can't breathe! I can't breathe!

Kacie drops to the floor beside me. My mom, who's entered seconds before, kneels on the floor, too.

"Deep breaths," says Kacie, rubbing my back. "It's okay. Cup your hands like this and take deep breaths."

Kacie cups her hands, takes a deep breath and exhales into her cupped hands. She does it again and again, and I mirror her.

"Good. That's good," she says. "Everything's going to be okay. One step at a time. Deep, easy, even breaths."

Eventually, I regain normal breathing, and Kacie leads me to an overstuffed burgundy chair.

A sea of flowers surrounds the two matching mahogany coffins. Carnations of every color. Red and yellow roses. Planters and baskets. They're everywhere, despite my request that, in lieu of flowers, donations be sent to a charity of choice. The floral smell overwhelms me. It hangs like a thick fog, and I feel queasy again.

I sniff and glance up, and the next three hours are a blur. I feel as if I'm on autopilot and watching someone else's movie. The line of people who want to pay their respects is a couple of hours long. I recognize most of them, but some I don't.

I see parents of children who attend Aiden's nursery school and can't stop the tears as the realization hits me that I will never take him there again, never watch him perform in the annual Christmas show, or buy a Halloween costume for the class party and parade.

I meet Tom's co-workers, including Pete, and they share stories I never heard. Most are about Tom pulling pranks on them, such as the time he taped over the sensor on his co-worker Bill's mouse, and Bill couldn't figure out why he could click but not scroll. It's typical Tom, always making others laugh.

"Tavi." Tom's mother, Deborah, places her tiny hand on my shoulder. "This is Tom's friend Eddie Horn. His family moved away when Tommy was ten. He lives in Ohio."

I force a slight smile. "Thank you for coming."

"I was in town on business when I heard about the accident," said Eddie, who looked as if he could be Tom's brother. He had the same thick, dark hair and brows. "I postponed my return so I could come and pay my respects. Tom and I sort of lost touch over the years, but I have so many wonderful memories of our childhood."

Again, I force a slight smile and steady myself for the next person in line—Tom's high school sweetheart, whom everyone expected him to marry. Beth broke his heart during Tom's first year in medical school when she dumped him for a man she worked with and later married. I remember the first time I met her.

"Which do you like better?" Tom held up two ties in the men's store at the shopping mall. Before I had a chance to answer, I heard, "The blue one." I turned around and saw a gorgeous woman with classic red hair, vibrant and attention-getting. She was stunning. Her legs went on forever, and she looked as if she'd just stepped off a photo shoot for a fashion magazine.

Tom lowered the two ties. "Beth." Tom walked over and put his arm around me. "Tav, this is Beth. Beth, this is my fiancée, Tavi."

Beth twisted her ruby lips into a smile that looked more like a smirk. "Oh! What a cute *little girl's* name!"

Tom pulled me closer.

Beth lifted her narrow shoulders slightly. "Well, congratulations. I hope you'll be as happy as William and I are."

"Thank you," I said. "I'm sure we'll be even happier than you and *Billy*. Oh, and what a cute *little boy's* name!"

Beth cleared her throat and managed a weak smile before tossing her hair back and sashaying away, her hips swaying back and forth in quarter time.

Tom chuckled. "I think that's the first time I've seen Beth speechless. She had no idea how to respond to your comment." He leaned toward me, and we kissed.

I hear Beth, but I don't. I know she's talking, but I'm in another place mentally. *Snap out of it, Tavi. Thank her for coming.* I glance at the two coffins, and a part of me wants to crawl inside and hold my baby boy. *Who will hold him in heaven? Who will be there to comfort him during a thunderstorm or when he has a bad dream?* I can't imagine my life without him.

"Please let me know if there's anything I can do," Beth says.

"Yes, yes, I will. Thank you for coming." *You are the last person in this world I would ask.*

By the time I see the last visitor, I'm emotionally and physically exhausted. I imagine I'm a worn mop that's falling apart, thinning strings unable to absorb the sorrow.

Surprisingly, Mom wasn't bad tonight. While she's never been overly affectionate with me, she's always been over-the-top with Aiden. I always felt as if she was trying to outdo me.

Mom walked into the house with an armful of packages. "Where's my boy?" she asked.

"Shush, Mom, he's napping."

"He still takes naps?"

"Yes, Mom. He still naps. He's only two."

Mom pouted. "You stopped taking naps when you were two. What did I do to deserve such a bratty kid?"

Mom placed her armful of gifts on the living room floor. "I picked him up a few things today."

"Looks like more than a few things, Mom. His birthday isn't for another two months."

She waved her hand. "Who says I can only buy my grandson gifts for his birthday? He's special, and a special boy deserves special gifts."

I forced a smile, thinking the only time Mom bought me gifts was for my birthday and Christmas. To this day, I'm convinced my dad was the one who shopped for me because Mom seemed just as surprised as I was when I opened my gifts. Once, I overheard her scolding Dad for spending too much.

"Will he be up soon?" she asked.

"Probably not for another hour."

"Then I'll run another errand and return. Don't let him open the gifts until I get back."

I suppose spending time with her daughter would've been too much to ask. As far as Mom was concerned, the only worthwhile thing I'd ever done was give her a grandson, the boy she had always hoped for.

"Are you ready to go?" Kacie asks.

I nod, unsure if I'll be able to move. I feel like a wet sponge, heavy with tears and emotions absorbed through countless exchanges during the last three hours.

Tom's mom, Deborah, and my mom walk out together. Tom's mom seems so old. Like me, Tom was an only child. His parents were twelve years apart, and they met through a work function when his mom was thirty-five. His dad never expected to be a father, but Deborah had told him she wanted at least one child. One child was all she got, and now he was gone, along with her only grandchild.

Kacie opens the car door, and I crawl in, recline the seat and close my eyes. She shuts my door and opens hers. I feel her eyes on me, but she doesn't speak. Instead, she puts the key in the ignition, and we head for my house. I'm grateful for the silence that follows. It's the kind of silence that comes from friends knowing friends. Nothing needs to be said. No one needs to be heard. Silence is a welcomed hug after a night of faces and condolences that forms a meteor of exhaustion.

"Do you want me to spend the night again or come in?" Kacie asks as she pulls into my driveway.

I shake my head. "I'll be okay. I'm going right to bed."

Kacie nods. "I'll be over early. Call me if you need anything."

I walk into an empty house, wondering how I will get through tomorrow. Tom's mom had a plot for six in the cemetery on the outskirts of town. When she offered to bury Tom and Aiden there, it seemed like the right thing to do.

I crawl into bed and pull up the sheet, tucking it under my chin. My eyes feel heavy, and I'm hopeful about the sleeping pill I've just taken. I reach over to where Tom would've been and wave my arm back and forth over the cool silk sheet.

Even though I could lie in the middle of the bed, I stay on my side. I used to love having the whole bed to myself when Tom worked overnight at the hospital. Now, I'd give anything to have him for just one more night. I wouldn't even nudge him for snoring or be annoyed by him rubbing his bare feet together under the covers. I'd lie perfectly still and not say a word.

I feel as though a stage curtain is closing on me while I'm standing in the middle, basking in the spotlight. Then suddenly the spotlight fades, and I'm in the dark, trying desperately to find my way to the other side of the curtain, but I can't. The curtain folds are intertwined, and I'm unable to find where the two ends separate.

My eyelids close, and I blink them open, not ready to succumb to the darkness just yet. I pick up the photo on my nightstand of Tom, Aiden and me. I remember the day it was taken.

Aiden was three and loved trains. Tom surprised him one weekend with an authentic steam train ride through the countryside. I'd never seen Aiden smile as much as he did that day. The photo is of the three of us standing in front of the steam engine. Many more steam train rides would follow, some requiring us to travel hours from home and spend the night in a hotel.

That Christmas, Tom bought Aiden his first "real" train set, and they put it around the Christmas tree. Aiden spent hours stretched out on his side, watching the train go 'round and 'round.

"Mommy, when I grow up, I'm going to drive trains," Aiden shouted.

My little boy will never grow up. Maybe he's driving trains in heaven.

I picture Aiden watching the train, his cheek resting on his open palm, supported by his bent arm and elbow on the floor.

I picture the train going around and around. My eyes get heavier and heavier. I fight to stay awake because I want to recall this moment in as much detail as I can.

Aiden wore pajamas with feet. Little red engines and the word "Choo-Choo!" were printed on them.

"You can't wear your pajamas to school."

He crossed his little arms and frowned. "No!"

"Aiden, come on. Miss Pam says you can wear your pajamas on Pajama Day. Today isn't Pajama Day."

"Why can't every day be Pajama Day?"

"Because it can't. Now come on. We're going to be late. If you don't take them off, we won't go on the train ride this weekend."

He sobbed as I removed the pajamas and dressed him in more appropriate school attire. But I felt like a terrible mother the rest of the day. What kind of mother threatens her toddler so that if he doesn't take off his pajamas to go to school, he'll be punished?

I felt lousy and later apologized to him. "It wasn't a very grown-up thing to do," I said.

"That's okay, Mommy. Grown-ups make mistakes, too."

I hear Kacie in the kitchen before my alarm, which I had set for eight. From the slivers of sunshine sneaking into my bedroom from the sides of my window shades, it looks like a beautiful day to have a funeral.

I shake my head, thinking back on all of the times I used that phrase for something I'd been looking forward to. It's a beautiful day to go to the park, for a picnic or for a bicycle ride. You never think of using the word beautiful in the same sentence as funeral. It seems incongruous.

"What's a word for inharmonious?" Tom asked me while poring over the Sunday crossword puzzle in the newspaper.

"How many letters?"

"Eleven. Starts with an 'I' and ends with an 'S.'"

"Incongruous."

"Darn!" Tom shook his head. "You are so much better at this than me."

"Well, I am the one with the English degree," I teased.

After showering, I traipse downstairs, and Kacie welcomes me with a mug of coffee and a blueberry muffin. "I stopped at the store on the way here," she says.

I take the mug and sit down. "I'm not hungry."

Kacie places the plate in front of me. "You have to eat something."

I know she's right, so I break a small piece off the muffin. Out of the corner of my eye, I see Kacie touch her stomach. "Everything okay?"

Kacie grins. "The baby kicked."

I pivot in my chair so quickly that I spill a little coffee. "You didn't tell me you felt the baby kick. Why didn't you tell me you felt the baby kick?"

Kacie cowers. "I wanted to. I was going to, but then all of this happened, and I didn't want to upset you."

I stand and hug Kacie. "Kacie, I'm happy for you. Please don't think you can't share things with me because they might upset me. I'm at the lowest I've ever been, but I still want to be there for you as much as I can. Please, don't shut me out."

Kacie begins to cry, which makes me cry, and we end up one big crying mess.

Tom and I were on vacation, and we pulled into a hotel for the night. It was mid-September, and we'd decided a road trip through the northeastern United States would be relaxing and a great way to see the beautiful colors of autumn.

After showering and dressing, I plopped into bed. That's when I felt this strange flutter. *Omigosh! Omigosh! Omigosh! Is that?* I felt it again and began to cry.

"Is everything okay?" Tom asked.

My eyes watered. "I just felt the baby."

Tom hugged me and whispered, "I love you, Tav. More and more each day."

I called Kacie right away. I cried. She cried. But they were tears of immeasurable joy. Finally, I was going to have the family I'd always wanted.

We're the first to arrive for the funeral service. I'm glad we're alone. I walk up to my baby boy's coffin and touch his little hands. They're cold and look like baby doll hands—so perfectly placed on top of his black suit jacket. His blond hair is parted and lies perfectly to one side. It's too perfect, and I instinctively pull a few small strands down over his forehead. *There, much better. Little boys don't have perfect hair.* I touch his tiny lips and they feel waxy.

Through my broken speech, I manage to talk to Aiden. "Hey, buddy. I can't go where you're going right now, but save a seat for me." I sniff. "You're the best thing that's ever happened to your dad and me. The *best* thing. And I will never forget you or stop missing you. But I'll see you again some day. I promise. I love you so much, Aiden."

I take a deep breath, and shuffle over to Tom's coffin and touch his hands, lingering on his gold wedding band. I lean over and kiss his lips. "Thank you, honey, for a wonderful life," I whisper. "You were so much more than I deserved. I don't know how I'm going to be able to go on without you. Take care of our little boy."

I turn and can't stop the tears. Kacie puts her arm around me and leads me to the same big, overstuffed chair I sat in the night before. Everyone else, besides Kacie, Mom and Tom's mom who are sitting next to me, sit on padded folding chairs. I feel queasy. Maybe the muffin was too much.

Kacie leans over. "Everything okay?"

I rub my belly. "Stomach doesn't feel quite right."

Kacie rummages in her purse and hands me a pill to help settle my stomach. I pool a puddle of saliva in my mouth and swallow the pill.

The minister walks in, and the service opens with a prayer. I bow my head and listen through a haze of grief so thick that his words pile on top of one another, and I can't make sense of them. I hear "Amen" and look up.

Kacie pulls into the cemetery behind the hearse carrying Tom and Aiden's coffins. Mom and Deborah are riding with us. I'm in a daze, feeling as if I'm watching everything that's going on from a distance. I know that my therapist would tell me I'm dissociating to numb my pain. I want to be in the present, but it's so painful.

I stare out the window as we pass grave after grave. Some of the gravesites have flowers on them. Others look lonely and forgotten. I silently pledge that I'll put flowers on Aiden and Tom's graves every week. I don't want them to be forgotten.

I'm thankful the ride is relatively peaceful, barring a few sniffles coming from the seat behind me.

Kacie stops, turns off the ignition, pulls out the key and turns to me. "You can do this. For Tom and Aiden. I won't leave your side."

I sit in front of the two coffins under a white canopy. The scalloped edges of the canopy sway slightly in the gentle breeze. Kacie, Mom and Deborah sit with me, and the others crowd around behind us.

Once again, the minister opens the service with a prayer. I feel as if that's all I've been doing lately, and I'm tired of praying and tired of my prayers not being answered.

I hear the minister say "green pastures" and "quiet waters," and I feel nauseous and inhale and exhale slowly to keep from vomiting.

"Let us close with a prayer," the minister says.

I bow my head, and the realization that I'll never be this physically close to Tom and Aiden ever again boils into a raging lament.

Freya

I listen to Mom explain why I'm in the hospital, surrounded by distracting beeping machines.

"You were in a car crash, Freya. You had some serious injuries. The doctors put you in a medically-induced coma to reduce the swelling and pressure on your brain."

"Where's Nate? I was with Nate."

"Yes, Nate was driving."

"I want to see him."

Mom cupped my hand in hers. "Freya, there's something I need to tell you. Nate didn't make it."

"What do you mean he didn't make it?"

"Nate's car hit another car, and Nate didn't survive the crash. A father and son in the other car died."

I shake my head, trying to make sense of what Mom is saying. The last thing I remember is fighting with Nate.

"I don't understand why you're so mad," I told Nate on our way home from school.

He hit the steering wheel with the palm of his hand. "I told you to stay away from him."

"That's sort of hard to do when he's my lab partner."

"Ask Mr. Simmons for a new lab partner. Tell him Tony makes you feel uncomfortable and that you'd prefer to have a girl for a lab partner."

I mustered the courage to disagree with Nate, something I rarely did because it made him angry.

"But he doesn't make me feel uncomfortable. We've been friends since kindergarten."

Nate gripped the steering wheel so tightly his knuckles turned white. He pushed the gas pedal down. "You're mine. I don't want him taking what's mine."

"You need to stop being so possessive," I said. "And you need to slow down."

"I'm only possessive because I love you and care about you so much. If you loved me as much as I love you, you'd ask for a new lab partner."

"That's not fair. I shouldn't have to prove my love to you by always doing what you want me to do."

Nate pushed down the gas pedal. "Has that worthless Emma been talking to you again? Putting stupid ideas into your head?" Nate looked over at me.

"Nate! Stop."

A surge of adrenalin courses through my veins. I feel queasy and light-headed. "No! No! It's not true."

Mom cups my hands and stares into my eyes. It's a serious stare, the kind that commands my attention. "It's true. I wish it wasn't, but it is. Nate ran through a stop sign. The police said he was speeding. Do you remember him going fast? Do you know why he wasn't paying attention?"

It's because of me. I distracted Nate, and he missed the stop sign. Oh, God! I made him kill that father and son. It was me. If I had just done what he wanted me to do, we wouldn't have been fighting. And if we hadn't been fighting, Nate wouldn't have gotten mad. And if Nate hadn't gotten mad, he would have been paying attention and seen the stop sign. It was my fault.

I sob in Mom's arms, wishing I'd been the one to die and not Nate. "Do his parents hate me?"

"No, of course not," Mom says. "Why would they hate you?"

Because I killed their son.

I shrug. "I was in the car with Nate, and I didn't die."

Mom brushes my hair away from my eyes. "And they are thankful for that. Losing Nate was terrible, but they are glad you survived."

Would they think otherwise if they knew I killed him?

"Where's..." My body trembles, and I can barely say the words. "Where's he buried?"

"In the large cemetery on the outskirts of town."

A nurse walks into the room. "Time to check your vitals."

Mom moves away from the bed. "I told Freya she gave us quite a scare."

The nurse smiles. "But she's doing great now."

I see Mom checking her watch.

"You don't have to stay with me, Mom."

I hear the voice before I see her walk into my room.

"Freya!" Emma holds a colorful balloon bouquet in one hand and a stuffed pink elephant with big ears in the other.

Mom stands and takes the bouquet and elephant so Emma can hug me.

"Emma's been here every day," Mom says. She ties the balloon bouquet to the rail at the foot of my hospital bed and places the big-eared elephant on the window sill. "Now that Emma is here, I'm going to grab some lunch."

As soon as Mom and the nurse leave, I tell Emma what happened before the crash.

"It's not your fault, Freya."

"I was trying to stand up to him. Trying to explain that I loved him and he had nothing to worry about.

That he was the only guy I wanted." An avalanche of tears follows.

Emma sits on my bed, reaches over, and places her hands on my shoulders, and turns me slightly so we are face to face. "You did nothing wrong. I know how much you loved Nate. He was your first real boyfriend. But he shouldn't have been jealous because your lab partner was a guy. He was becoming way too possessive, and you know it."

"But I didn't want him to die."

"No, of course not. You just wanted him to understand how he was making you feel. You wanted him to loosen his reins on you. You needed some freedom."

"But I would've kept doing what he wanted me to do if it meant he wouldn't die."

"But that wouldn't have been living for you," Emma said. "Look what happened the weekend before the accident when you wanted to go to the mall with me."

"You care more about Emma than you do about me," Nate yelled.

I reached over to touch his arm, but he swatted it away.

"Don't. Touch. Me," he growled.

"But I never get to see Emma or my friends anymore."

"So, you'd rather spend time with them instead of me?"

"No, I'm not saying that."

"That's what I'm hearing. Besides, you didn't ask me before you agreed to go to the mall with her. You know you're supposed to ask me if you want to do something."

"But I didn't think you'd mind. She's my best friend."

"I thought I was your best friend."

"You're my boyfriend. And I love spending time with you, but I miss spending time with Emma."

"I'll let you go, but you must call me when you get to the mall and when you leave. You must also keep a list of everyone you talk to and see."

"Don't you trust me?"

"You don't deserve my trust. In fact, you don't deserve me. Have you looked in a mirror lately? You'll never be able to find anyone else who would date you."

I looked down at my hands. I used to have beautiful nails, but they were nothing but ragged stumps, accompanied by bloody cuticles from my obsessive chewing on them. "I'll keep a list. And I'll call you when I get to the mall and when we leave."

"Good," Nate said. "And we'll go over the list afterward."

I stared out the window and raised my hand to my eye. I yanked out an eyelash. I was trapped.

"You're stronger than you think, Freya. I can't even imagine what you're feeling, but please don't let your guilt become your prison. You'll get through this. I'll help you."

I nod. "When I get out, I want to see his parents. And where he's buried. Will you go with me?"

Emma manages a half-smile. "Of course."

"Did you go to Nate's funeral?"

Emma nodded. "Most of the class went."

"Probably everyone wished I'd died and not Nate."

"Don't even think that!" Emma said. "It was a terrible accident, and everyone's glad you survived. No one blames you. Nate was driving too fast. How many times has he driven down that road, taking you home? He knew there was a stop sign there, but he was too absorbed in arguing with you about having a male lab partner. It was a stupid argument and an accident that didn't need to happen."

I sighed. "I remember when we first started dating. I felt special and loved because Nate couldn't seem to live a moment without hearing from me."

"Yes," Emma said. "But you started to realize that he was taking you away from everyone you loved. His possessiveness stopped you from living your own life. You even quit the cheerleading squad for him."

Nate and I had just left the movie theater and were headed to get milkshakes.

He slipped his arm around me as we walked to the car. "I've been thinking that you should quit cheerleading."

I abruptly turned to face him, and his arm fell to his side. "What? You must be kidding. I worked my butt off to make the squad. Why would I want to quit?"

Nate's shoulders and head sank. "To make me happy."

I shook my head in disbelief. "You're not serious?"

"I don't like other guys looking at you. You wear that cheerleading uniform, and sometimes when you jump, your skirt comes up."

"But I have shorts under my skirt. It's not like they see anything."

"But I know what guys are thinking. They think you're loose and want to be with you. And I love you too much to have other guys think badly about you."

"But it's good exercise, and I love it."

"Do you love it more than me?"

Mom walks in carrying a magazine. "Did I give you girls enough time to catch up?"

Emma checks her watch. "I could stay and talk to my bestie all night long, but I have to get to work."

Emma works part-time as a clerk in a grocery store.

"My shift starts in thirty minutes, and I have to stop and get gas. Dad doesn't like when the tank is so close to empty."

"Thanks for coming, Em."

She flashed me a thumbs-up. "See you tomorrow."

"Did you and Emma have a good visit?" Mom asks.

I reach for the drink on my nightstand and take a sip. "Yeah."

Mom sits on the chair.

I scrape my lower lips with my front teeth, weighing whether I want to know the answer to the question on the tip of my tongue. "Did Dad visit me?"

Mom sat up straighter. "Yes, of course he did. He was really worried about you."

I'm not sure whether to believe Mom. My entire life, she's made excuses for my deadbeat dad. He's always been more absent than present. They divorced when I was two. Mom never remarried, but Dad's on his third wife. Sabrina isn't too bad, except for the fact that she could be my older sister. "Does he know I'm going home in a couple of days?"

Mom rubs her neck as if it helps her think. "I'll call him tonight and let him know."

"Mom, you look tired. Go home and get some rest. I'll be fine."

Mom yawns. "Are you sure?"

"I'm sure."

Mom leaves, and I pick up the magazine she left behind. I flip through the pages, but everything is a blur. I can't stop thinking about Dad. I pick up my cell phone, which survived the crash, and that Mom left on my nightstand. I consider calling him. But why should I? I'm the one in the hospital, fortunate to be alive.

My therapist tells me I struggle with fear of abandonment, and I'd rather be in a dysfunctional relationship than alone. Deep down inside, I know she's right, but I don't know how to overcome this fear.

The nurse stops in, and I ask for something to help me sleep. She checks my chart and tells me she'll be right back.

I scroll through the photos on my cell phone. There are hundreds of pictures of Nate and me. At the beach. Prom. Amusement park. Skiing. Hiking. Washing Nate's car. I put the phone down, and bury my face in my pillow and scream.

"Do you think it will always be like this?" I asked Nate at our six-month anniversary. "I've never been this happy."

Nate picked up a French fry. "No," he paused.

My hands flew to my heart, fearful that he was going to tell me he didn't want to date me anymore.

"It's going to be better." Nate's eyes widened, and a big, sloppy grin couched in a five o'clock shadow took up most of his face. "A year from now, two years from now, you'll be even more mine."

I breathed a sigh of relief. I'd never felt so loved and wanted. Maybe Dad didn't think I was worth having, but Nate did.

The nurse returns, and I take the sleeping pills. As I teeter between sleep and consciousness, I ask myself a million why's.

Why did Nate and I have to fight?

Why couldn't I just do what Nate wanted me to do?

Why did I pick that moment to push back?

Why couldn't we have arrived at that intersection and gone through the stop sign five minutes later when there was no car to hit?

Why? Why? Why?

But mostly, why did I survive and Nate didn't?

My cell phone rings. It's Dad, and I don't want to talk to him. Instead, I close my eyes, hoping that I can quiet the noise in my brain. He leaves a voicemail, and I listen to it.

"Hey, Frey. It's Dad. Talked to your mom tonight. She says you're doing well. Ugh. Yeah. I stopped in to see you. Anyway, I must go. Got a poker game tonight. Take care."

I listen to the voicemail a couple more times, hoping that I missed an "I love you" or "I was worried sick about you"—anything that would show an ounce of love. He only called because Mom begged him to.

Despite taking sleeping pills, I toss and turn. Flashbacks from the accident play a loop in my head. I see Nate's angry face and shudder as he slams his palm against the steering wheel. I hear crunching metal and taste blood in my mouth before sinking into darkness. I wonder if I will ever be able to forget, or more importantly, forgive myself.

I wake up exhausted, and minutes later, my breakfast is delivered. I stare at the eggs, bacon and toast, and I burst into tears because I realize that Nate will never eat eggs, bacon and toast ever again.

My phone rings, and I check the ID before answering. "Hi, Mom."

"How are you this morning, sweetie?"

"Tired."

"Didn't sleep well then?"

"No."

"Did you ask for something?"

"Yes, but it didn't work. I just couldn't stop thinking about the crash, or at least what I remember."

"I'm talking to the doctor later, and I'll ask him if I can bring you home a day early. You'll sleep better in your own bed."

I pick up my fork and move the food around on the plate, so it looks like I ate some of it. "That sounds good. I want to go home."

Splice

Tavi

It's been a week since we buried Tom and Aiden. I visit their graves every day. I clear away the dead flowers and replace them with bouquets I buy at the grocery store.

"You're here a lot."

My hand flies to my chest, and I look up and see an older lady wearing a black sweatsuit with pink stripes down the side of the pants and sleeves.

"I'm sorry," she says. "I didn't mean to startle you."

I stand. "That's okay. I'm just not used to seeing people here."

She smiles. "I'm nearby. I'm Lena."

I manage a slight wave. "I'm Tavi."

She purses her lips. "Tavi. What a beautiful name!"

"Thanks. Lena's pretty, too."

She points toward the graves. "Sorry for your loss."

I nod. "Thank you."

"If you ever want to talk... Well, I'm a good listener. And I'm here every day."

I wave as Lena walks away, wondering if she, too, lost someone dear who is buried here.

My cell phone rings. "Hi, Kacie."

"Where are you?" she asks. "I stopped by with a latte and bagel from your favorite shop."

"I'm just leaving the cemetery. Just let yourself in. You know where the key is. I'll be home in ten."

I walk in the door and find Kacie folding the wash I'd left in the dryer. "You don't have to do that."

"It's no biggie," she says, snapping my white shorts before folding them. "Remember the time we snuck into my parents' wine cellar and took a bottle of red wine?"

I smile. I remember.

"Mom and Dad won't know," Kacie said. "They have so much wine in here, they'll never miss one bottle."

Kacie and I took a bottle of red wine and escaped to her bedroom, where we took turns guzzling it. I ended up throwing up and getting red wine all over my white shorts. We washed the shorts twice but couldn't get the red stain out. And we ended up being wrong about her parents not missing the wine.

It turned out Kacie's parents separated their wine into A, B and C bottles. An "A" bottle of wine was the most expensive, followed by B and C bottles. They drank the C bottles when they'd already had too much to drink. As her mom later explained, they didn't want to waste an "A" bottle of wine if they were too drunk to appreciate it.

Unfortunately for us, Kacie had selected an "A" bottle. It was a merlot from Tuscany and cost $891. Her parents had just received the shipment and knew immediately that a bottle was missing.

I put my latte in the microwave to reheat it. "Thanks for bringing this over."

"I'm worried about you," Kacie says. "Maybe you shouldn't go to the cemetery every day."

I sit down beside Kacie at the kitchen island. "But it's where they are, where I feel the closest to them. It's like I'm in a thick fog, and I can't find my way out. I keep waiting for it to lift, but it's a cloak I can't seem to escape from."

"Are you still seeing your therapist?"

I hug my coffee cup with both hands. "Yes, and it helps. Sort of."

"What about checking out a grief group? Joan said it really helped her when her mother died."

I shake my head. "I'm not sure a grief group is for me. I think listening to everyone else talk about their losses would depress me."

"Not to change the subject, but are you going to Diana's party on Saturday? Getting out might be good for you."

"I don't know. I don't want everyone to feel as though they have to walk on eggshells for fear of saying the wrong thing to me. And I'll be the only one there without a spouse."

Tom and I had planned to attend Diana's 40th birthday party. She was the cooler, older sister Kacie and I never had. I met Diana when she offered to host Kacie's bachelorette party at her beach condo. At the time, they worked together.

"Don't be silly," Kacie says. "Whenever we get together, the guys always end up in one room and the girls in the other. Besides, you haven't met Diana's new boyfriend yet."

"I just don't think I'm up for being around couples."

Kacie sighs. "Okay, but if you don't go to Diana's party, then will you go shopping with me tomorrow? I need new bras, and you know how much I hate shopping for bras. Remember the Great Bra Fiasco?"

I nod. "How could I ever forget that?"

I waited for Kacie outside the dressing room at one of our favorite stores.

"I really, really like this bra," Kacie said. "It's a perfect fit. But I don't see a tag anywhere."

"I'm sure the cashier can look up the code."

Kacie walked out of the dressing room. "This was the only one on the rack. I'll see if they can order me two more."

The clerk looked at the bra and then at Kacie. "You found this bra on one of our racks?"

Kacie nodded. "And I'd like to order more, if that's possible."

The woman shook her head. "I'm sorry. This isn't our bra."

I'd been looking at panties on a nearby rack when I heard what the clerk said. I walked over. "Are you saying that Kacie tried on a bra that belonged to someone else?"

"I'm afraid so," the clerk said. "It's a swap. It happens sometimes."

"Eww!" Kacie screeched. "How gross! I need to go home and shower!"

"Okay, I'll go bra shopping. But you have to promise to visit the pet store with me."

"Are you still thinking about getting a puppy?" Kacie asks. "I figured that… Well, you know, with Aiden gone…"

"I know we were going to surprise Aiden with a puppy on his birthday, but I was thinking it might be good for me. It would keep me company and force me to exercise because I'd need to take it for walks."

"You could look into rescuing a dog. My sister-in-law rescued her dog, and she's a sweetheart."

"I'll think about it."

Kacie looks at her phone. "I need to run. I'll call you later."

"Mom and I are going out to dinner."

Kacie's eyes widen.

"I know. I surprised myself when I accepted her invitation."

"Maybe it won't be that bad," Kacie says. "She seems like she's trying to be nice."

"That's just it, Kace. She shouldn't have to try. I'm her daughter."

Mom stepped out of the black silk dress and tossed it on her bed. It was the third dress she had tried on that day, and they were all too tight.

"It's all your fault, Tavi. If I wouldn't have had you, I'd still be a size six."

I looked up from the floor where I was playing with my doll. My chin jiggled and tears formed in my eyes. "I'm sorry, Mommy."

"Ugh. Sorry's not good enough. Not only did you take my figure away, you stole my husband."

"Daddy? I didn't steal Daddy."

"Ugh. Get out of here. Go play in your room. I don't want you in my sight."

I picked up my dolly, and went to my room and cried. *Why does Mommy hate me, Dolly? Why did she blame me for her dress not fitting? Why did she blame me when the dryer broke?*

I walk into Aiden's room and see all the things he loved—his wooden train set, superhero action figures, building blocks and so many tiny metal cars they have spilled out of a plastic bin and onto the floor.

I run my fingers across the spines of books on the shelf next to his bed. I pull one out and open it to a dog-eared page that Aiden had scribbled on with red crayon.

I breathe in deeply and exhale. I feel empty inside, like I've plunged into an inner abyss that, despite clawing my way, I'm unable to escape. The darkness surrounds me, and as much as I try to break through the surface, I can't reach it. There are too many toys, too many books, too many of Aiden's things.

I scan the room. It's the perfect space for a little boy. Colorful train prints, which had replaced prints of woodland animals on the walls, match the comforter on his bed. *Do I leave everything like this? Do I give everything away?* I wonder what Tom would have done.

I pick up a wooden toy train engine and turn it over in my hand. I close my eyes and picture Aiden's hand on the toy engine, pushing it around and around the wooden track and making train whistle sounds.

I feel guilty that I didn't buy him the new train engine the last time we went shopping.

"Please, mommy, please."

"Not today, Aiden. You have a birthday coming up. Why not ask for it for your birthday?"

"But I want it now. Can't I have it now?"

"Mommy doesn't have the money to buy it now. Maybe for your birthday."

We always think there will be a tomorrow. But sometimes there isn't a tomorrow. There's only today.

I close Aiden's bedroom door, walk to my room and open my closet. Half of the closet contains my clothing and the other half Tom's. While my half is organized according to seasons, his side is a mishmash of garments. I have so many clothes that the rod buckles in the middle.

I'll have the whole closet for just my things. As soon as I think it, I'm overcome with guilt. *That's an insensitive thing to think!*

I slam the closet door shut. Maybe I should see if Tom's mother would like any of his clothes. I've read stories about people who save a piece or two of a loved one's clothing and wear them to feel closer to the deceased.

"What do you think?" Tom asked, emerging from the men's dressing room.

He's wearing blue jeans and a blue button-down shirt.

"Pull out the shirt," I said. I reached up and unbuttoned the first two buttons. "It looks way too stuffy."

"Really?"

"Really. Trust me. Now, doesn't that feel better?"

He stretched his neck like a turtle. "Much better."

"Told you."

I pull out the button-down shirt and hang it in my closet in the corner. I look for another item or two with special meaning and settle on a worn cable-knit sweater with holes in the elbows and a sweatshirt from his alma mater. Both have seen better days, but that's why I choose them. They were loved and worn.

I smell the sweater, drinking in the woodsy smell of his cologne. I put on the sweater, lie down on my bed and curl up like a cat, knees to my chest and arms crossed. I feel as though Tom is hugging me, and I lay there for a few minutes, enjoying the warmth of the sweater and the closeness I feel to Tom.

I glance at the clock on the nightstand. I need to get ready to meet Mom. I consider canceling our dinner date. She probably wouldn't care. She might even feel relieved.

I jump into the shower and lean forward so the water is hitting my face. I reach down to turn the knob. I like hot water. Not too hot that it scalds my skin, but hot enough that I feel as if I'm getting clean.

I throw on my favorite jeans and an animal-print camisole and cardigan. I lean in toward the bathroom mirror and notice the dark circles under my eyes. I haven't been sleeping well, and it shows.

I open my vanity drawer and pull out my under-eye concealer. I wonder if I'll ever sleep through the night again.

Mom looks at her watch as I enter the restaurant. "About time you get here."

"I thought you said six."

"I said 5:45," she says in a staccato voice.

"Oh, sorry."

"You should be glad I waited."

"Like I said, sorry I had the time wrong."

"It's just like you not to pay attention to anything I say."

I want to leave. Mom has already made me feel like crap, and we've only been together for thirty seconds.

"No, we might as well eat now that *you're* here." She emphasizes "you're" and it's like another slap in the face.

Okay. I hear you, Mom. It's all my fault. I close my eyes and take a deep breath, exhaling slowly.

"Well, are you coming?"

I open my eyes and see Mom waiting for me at the check-in podium.

We are escorted to a table in the middle of the restaurant.

Mom sits down. "Wish we had a booth. Maybe if you'd been on time, we might've gotten a booth."

I take the menu from the server. "And maybe not."

"Would you prefer to wait for a booth?" the server asks.

Mom shakes her head. "No, I've waited long enough."

I don't feel much like eating, but I order a bowl of tomato bisque. For the next hour, I'm held captive by Mom's passive-aggressive behavior. I don't know why I think she will ever change. When we're with other people, she acts normal, but when we're alone, she becomes a different person. Everything is my fault.

I'm surprised she hasn't blamed me for Tom and Aiden's deaths. I've been expecting her to criticize me for being home sick instead of in the car with them. Maybe I could've prevented it. Maybe I would've seen the car and yelled for Tom to stop. I've thought about the what-ifs over and over, but the truth is I'll never know. Maybe when your time is up, it's up.

I sip my coffee and watch Mom eat a slice of apple pie. I silently congratulate myself for making it through dinner.

I watch as the hostess seats a family in a booth nearby. Mom, Dad and two small children who appear to be a couple of years apart in age. Tom and I had been trying to get pregnant for the last half year but hadn't had any luck. I suddenly realize that I don't remember having my period recently. With everything that has happened, I'd lost track of it. I make a mental note to check the calendar when I get home. I always mark the date I get my period with a "P" on the calendar in our office and circle it.

"Are you ready?" Mom asks.

I nod. I offer to pay the check even though Mom has invited me to dinner, and she doesn't argue. She leaves the tip.

We walk out of the restaurant together but immediately head for our cars on opposite sides of the parking lot.

There's no hug. No "Let's do this again soon." I don't know why I think she will ever change.

Freya

I walk into my bedroom, and everything looks the same but it feels different. *I* feel different.

It once bothered me that my bedroom furniture was a collection of cheap pieces Mom bought at the discount store. I'm ashamed that something so stupid bothered me so much. So what if I used stacked plastic crates for a nightstand? Who cares that two of my dresser drawer knobs are missing and the mirror is cracked in the corner? All the things that once mattered seem so insignificant.

I throw myself on my bed and grab the brown bear I've had since I was a baby. The bear is disfigured, having lost some of its stuffing. I trace the stitches that Mom made to keep him whole. He's lost an eye and half of his stitched smile. I pull him in and hold him close to my heart. My chin trembles as I prepare for another avalanche of tears. I'm falling apart like my bear.

I reach over and pick up the photo of Nate and me at the prom sitting on my plastic crate nightstand. I stare at Nate, trying to remember every detail of that night.

I kissed Mom goodbye, and Nate and I left for the prom. As soon as we got in his car, the yelling began.

"I can't believe you picked that dress," he shouted. "You look like a hooker."

My shoulders sank. "But I love this dress. Everyone is wearing two-pieces this year."

Nate pulled away from the house. "But you're not everyone. You're *my* girlfriend, and I get to say what you wear. I'll let it go this time, but the next time you better check with me to make sure I approve."

I gulped. "I saved months to buy this dress."

"Like I said, I'll let it go this time."

I stared at the white rose corsage wristlet he gave me before we left. It looked so pretty on my arm and completely hid the bruise I'd gotten after Nate grabbed my wrist too hard while I was talking to a group of students that included boys.

I put the photo back on the nightstand and head to the bathroom to freshen up before Emma arrives. She's always early and hates to be late for anything, even something as unpleasant as going to a cemetery.

I hear Emma yell for me from downstairs and I find her lounging on the couch and flipping through a magazine. She holds up the magazine and points to a page containing before and after photos of a girl's hairstyle. "I love this shorter style."

"I need to do something with my hair. Nate would never let me cut it." As soon as I spoke, I regretted it.

"I know I shouldn't speak ill about the dead, but that's another example of how Nate controlled you," Emma says.

I flipped down the car visor and opened the mirror. "I hate my hair. I'm thinking about getting it cut."

Nate reached over and flipped up the visor.

"Hey, I'm trying to put lip gloss on."

"You don't need lip gloss, and you don't need a new hairstyle. I like your long hair."

"So, you don't think I'd look pretty in short hair? Maybe just to my shoulders."

"No. Leave it like it is."

I cowered in my seat as Nate pulled away from the house. I could never do what I wanted to do anymore.

Emma jumps up from the couch. "Sorry. I didn't mean to upset you. Especially today."

I grab a tissue from the end table and blow my nose. "It's okay. You're right. I hate that you're right, but you are."

Emma grabs her purse from the couch. "Ready?"

I nod.

We pull away from the house, and I rub my stomach.

"You okay?"

"Every time I ride in a car since the accident, I get queasy," I explain. "It'll pass."

We pass the supermarket and gas station and stop at the red light. "Is there another way to get to the cemetery?"

Emma looks at me. "This is the shortest way."

"But is there *another* way?"

Emma turns off her right-turn signal. "We can go straight and turn down Plymouth."

I breathe a sigh of relief. "Thanks. I'm not ready to tackle the intersection where it happened."

"Are you still having flashbacks?" Emma asks.

"Yes. Mostly at night."

I play with my necklace as we pass through a river of graves. "There are so many."

My voice cracks, and I can't stop the tears. I bury my head in the palms of my hands and sob.

I unwrapped Nate's birthday present. "It's beautiful."

"That's a real diamond."

I touch the small sparkle in the center of a silver heart and take the necklace out of the gold foil box.

"Here, let me help."

I hand Nate the necklace and turn my back toward him, holding up my hair. "The chain is so dainty."

"Glad you like it."

"I love it. I will wear it forever."

I barely notice that Emma has parked the car. She reaches over and touches my arm. I sniff and ball up my tissue, putting it with the others, forming a mountain in my purse. I grab another handful of tissues before getting out of the car.

Emma and I walk arm in arm to the grave, which is still covered by a heap of flowers, most of which are dead. I touch my necklace, fall to my knees and sob. I can barely speak, but I want Nate to know how sorry I am.

Emma crouches next to me and rubs my back as I stumble through the words. "Sorry. So sorry. I'll never be able to..." My sobs grow louder. "...forgive myself. It's my fault. All my fault."

I feel the sun beat down on top of my head and shoulders, and it makes me cry even more to know that Nate will never feel the sun again. He's buried in a deep, dark hole. I should be in that hole.

I hear a strange voice. "Is there anything I can do?"

I look up and see an older woman wearing a black sweatsuit with pink stripes down the side of the pants and sleeves.

"I killed him. I killed my boyfriend."

I sob, and Emma hugs me. "That's not true, Freya."

The woman kneels next to me and stares right into my eyes. "Your friend's right. You shouldn't blame yourself."

"But we were fighting and..."

"Focusing on guilt instead of grief isn't good," she says. "Think about your family and friends who love you and how devastated they'd be if they had lost you."

I nod. "I'll try."

The woman smiles and stands up. "Practice seeing your survival as a gift. Focusing on guilt instead of grief will lead to nowhere you want to go."

As she walks away, I call out, "What's your name?"

"Lena."

I watch Lena until I can't see her anymore.

"She's right," Emma says. "You have to stop feeling guilty."

I pull up my T-shirt and wipe my wet cheeks. "I tell myself that, but at night when I'm alone in bed, I see Nate's bloody face. It plays a loop in my mind."

I touch the scar on my forehead right beneath the hairline on the right. "Every time I look into the mirror, I see this scar. It's a lasting reminder of that night and what I lost."

Emma rubs my back.

I heave. "I'm sorry, I'm such a mess."

"You're not a mess," Emma says. "It's just going to take some time."

We walk back to the car, and I open the door.

"Do you know where they're buried?" I can't say the words father and son, but Emma understands the question and points down the hill. "Can we stop there?"

"Are you sure that's a good idea?"

"Yeah, I..." I inhale deeply and exhale, letting the air tickle my lips. "I need to."

Standing in front of the two graves side by side, a million questions bombard my mind. Were they in pain? What was the last word each of them said? Did he cry for his mommy? *Stop it. Stop it. Freya!* But I can't stop thinking about Nate and the two buried beneath me. "I should be in the ground. Not them."

Once again, I burst into tears, and Emma tries to comfort me, but I push her arm away. I want to hurt. I need to hurt. I want to be punished for what I did. I pull out an eyebrow hair. Then another.

Emma slaps my hand. "Stop that! You don't want to end up like Mrs. Douglas and have to draw on your eyebrows."

"Okay, okay." I shove my hands into my pockets and head toward the car.

"Do you want to stop for coffee on the way home?" Emma asks.

"A vanilla and caramel Frappuccino sounds heavenly."

As soon as I say heavenly, I feel as though a thick, wiry rope has lassoed my heart and is pulling it as tightly as it can. I rub my chest to ease the physical pain.

Emma notices and quickly changes the conversation to the must-have items on her birthday list, which include a new cell phone and laptop.

"Don't pull into that spot," I shout.

Emma slams on the brakes. "Why not? It's the closest one to the door."

"Park over there. Next to that black Jeep."

Emma shakes her head and puts the car in reverse.

Nate pulled into the coffee shop. "Lucky for us getting a spot so close to the door."

We get out of the car. "Remember, it's my treat," I told him.

When we got to the counter, Nate ordered a vanilla Frappuccino with whipped cream and sprinkles. I did, too.

"Are you sure getting the whipped cream is a good idea?" he asked me.

I shrugged. "Why not? It's the best part of the drink."

Nate stared at my midsection. "I was just thinking you could skip the whipped topping."

The cashier's eyes widened. I felt my face heat up. I really, really, really wanted the whipped topping and sprinkles, but the way Nate looked at me made me feel as though I was an elephant.

"On second thought, no whipped topping or sprinkles for me."

"What are you getting?" Emma asks.

"A vanilla Frappuccino with whipped cream and sprinkles."

Emma heads for the table in the corner.

"No, let's sit here."

"First the parking spot, and now the table. Are you okay?"

I sit down. "Certain things evoke memories of Nate that are hard for me to deal with."

"Do you want me to pick you up for school on Monday?"

"I'm not sure I want to go back."

Emma jerks her head. "What? We only have a month left."

"I know, but I'm not sure if I'll be able to handle it. People staring and talking about me behind my back."

"I'll be there. No one is going to talk trash about you. They are probably more afraid of you than you are of them. No one wants to say or do the wrong thing. Everyone knows how difficult this has been for you."

I suck up the last of my Frappuccino, a mixture of icy goodness swirled with whipped topping that's turned into a creamy liquid.

When we get home, Dad's waiting for me on the front porch.

"Hey, Frey. I just thought I'd drop by to see how you are."

Emma waves goodbye and heads for work while I join Dad. Mom won't be home for another half hour.

I sit down beside Dad on a lawn chair that's seen better days. The webbing on the front left corner is no longer attached to the mental frame, and Mom's attempt at fixing it is a strip of clear packaging tape.

"Mom, what are you doing? Why don't you just buy a new chair?"

I watched as Mom cut a piece of clear packaging tape, attached it to the webbing and wrapped it around the metal frame.

"A new chair costs money. Besides, I can fix this one. You'll see. It'll be just like new."

The packaging tape held for a while, until it didn't.

I wrap the packaging tape around the metal frame, hoping there is some stickiness left. But it's of no use. It doesn't hold.

"Freya," Dad says. "I've come by because I wanted to tell you in person that I'm leaving."

I squint, trying to process what he's saying. He's never really been present, so leaving should be no big deal. Still...

"Where are you going?"

Dad cracks his neck and looks out toward the street. "Sabrina and I are headed south."

"South? What's south?"

Finally, Dad glances my way. "Her cousin knows someone who knows someone who needs help running a remodeling business. It's better money than I'm making now. Figured I might as well give it a shot."

I listen as Dad rambles on about this new job. "I'm leaving in a few days, so I wanted to come by and tell you."

I grab the arms of my chair. "A few days?"

"Yeah, heading out on Saturday." He reaches into his jeans pocket and pulls out a piece of paper with ragged edges. "Here, this is my new address. Same phone number, just a new address."

I take the piece of paper and fold it up into a tiny square.

"Sorry, I won't be here for your graduation."

You've never been here for much of anything.

"That's okay. It's just another day." *Like my birthday, which you always seem to forget.*

I watch as Dad pulls away in his pickup truck, knowing that I will probably never see or hear from him again. *You could've fixed this damn chair before you left. After all, you like remodeling!*

I sit on the porch until Mom comes home, trying to find my way back to happy moments spent with my dad. There are few.

"Just one more dollar," Dad told Mom. "I want to try to win Frey that big stuffed giraffe in the corner."

Mom handed Dad another dollar. "One more, and that's it. We need to eat for the week."

Dad picked up the softball and hurled it at the stacked milk bottles. They wobbled but didn't fall.

Dad's eyes narrowed, and he called the carnival worker over. "Mind if I check out your milk bottles?" he asked. "See, my little girl here wants that big giraffe, and I'm wondering if the milk bottles are solid wood. Maybe there's lead in them, eh?"

The carnival worker smirked. "Nah, but I tell you what. You just spent twenty bucks playing this game. I'll give your little one the giraffe."

Mom gets out of her car, rushes to the porch and hugs me. "How'd it go?"

She wants to know about my visit to the cemetery, but I'm not in the mood to talk about it. "Dad's leaving."

Mom sits on the wobbly chair next to me. "He told me earlier today when he called to tell me he was coming over."

"I guess he's not really leaving since he's never really been here in the first place," I say.

Mom listens but doesn't respond. She's never said a bad word about my dad, although she'd have every right to.

"Everyone he has ever dated or married has been more important than me," I say. "His own daughter."

Mom reaches over and takes my hand in hers. "I wish he would've been a better father. But I'm done making excuses for him. You're old enough to know the truth, and the truth is he wasn't much of a father. He wasn't much of a husband, either. I always thought we were better off without him."

I heave, and the sound crescendos into a sobbing lament. I hate my sperm donor. That's all he's ever been.

"Daddy, will you come to my birthday party?"

"You know how important you are to me, but that's the weekend I'm going on a fishing trip with the boys. I'll make it up to you. I promise."

I hung up the phone and looked at Mommy. "Daddy can't come."

Mommy opened her arms, and I flew into them.

"Why doesn't Daddy love me?"

"Oh, sweetie. He loves you. He's just not very good at being a Daddy."

Tavi

I kneel and place the flowers I bought on the graves. I wonder if I'll ever think less about their deaths and more about their lives.

"Hi, Tavi."

I stand up. "Hi, Lena. It's a beautiful day for a walk."

"It is, indeed. Would you like to join me?"

"Yes," I say, surprising myself that I answered so quickly. "I could use a walk."

We walk in silence for a few seconds before Lena speaks. "My son died when he was five."

"So, you know how I feel."

Lena nods. "I don't think you ever get over the loss of a child."

"Does it ever get easier?" I ask.

Lena sighs. "The loss of a child is a heavy burden you carry for the rest of your life. It never goes away, and you really can't just set it aside. But eventually, it becomes lighter to carry."

"Lighter?" I ask.

"It's like going on a hike with a backpack," she explains. "Initially, when you put on the backpack loaded with water and supplies for the day, it feels so very, very heavy, and you wonder how you will ever make it carrying that pack.

"But you do. After walking some time with the backpack, it still weighs the same, but you become more accustomed to carrying it. You learn how it is most comfortable to carry, and adjust along the way. You will learn, too."

I sigh. "I'm not sure I'll ever be able to get over this."

"Don't be too hard on yourself," Lena says. "Each person's grief journey is as unique as their fingerprint. We all process grief at different speeds and in different ways. The grief journey doesn't end in a week, a month or even a year. Don't let others' expectations be a guideline for your progress."

I stop walking and look around, noticing another new gravesite piled high with flowers up the hill from where we are. I glance at my watch. "I should turn back. But will I see you tomorrow?"

"I'll be here," Lena says, waving goodbye.

I pull into the driveway and wonder what it would be like living somewhere else. Maybe I should sell the house, although I remember that Tom once told me that if anything happened to him, I shouldn't be in a hurry to make any big decisions.

"I'm just saying, Tav, that if I die..."

"Stop it. I don't want to talk about you dying."

Tom put his hands on my shoulders and lifted my chin so that we were face-to-face. I hated his serious expression, but I also knew that if I didn't listen to what he had to say, he'd keep badgering me until I did.

"If anything ever happens to me, don't be in a rush to sell the house or make any other big life decisions."

"But I wouldn't want to live in this house without you."

"Maybe, and maybe not," Tom said. "But you should delay that decision for at least six months. Give yourself time."

I get the mail and walk into the house, leafing through the pieces. I stop and stare at the envelope and burst into tears. It's the lump-sum payout from the insurance company. Instead of opening it, I put it on the table. I'm not sure I'm ready to see lives reduced to dollars and cents.

The doorbell rings, and I open the door to find two kids selling candy bars for school. The last thing I want is chocolate, but I buy two anyway. I watch as the kids walk to the next house. Aiden will never sell candy bars for school. He will never even go to school. I realize in that instance that I've lost Aiden's future—what might have been. I hadn't quite thought about it like that.

I close the door and flop on the couch. I feel so alone, and I know I have to make some changes. Tom would be angry if I became a shell of my former self, and I feel it happening. Each day, I lose a little more of myself. *Go to the gym. Look for a job. Volunteer. Do something.*

It's in that moment of clarity that I realize I have to change. Holding on to yesterday will only lead to more sorrow and a never-ending spiral of destruction. I need to do better, not only for myself, but also for Tom and Aiden.

I immediately get up, grab a notepad and pen and begin to write:

Get a job
Volunteer
Go to gym

Consider getting a puppy

My cell phone rings. "Hi, Kacie. I saw you called earlier, but I was walking with Lena."

"Lena?"

"I met her at the cemetery. She's an older woman who walks through the cemetery every day."

"Oh. Well, anyway, I was just calling to tell you I'll pick you up after work. Say around 5?"

"The time works, but I'll drive. I want to stop at the cemetery first, and then I'll be over to pick you up."

"Okay. Anything else happen today?"

"I'm thinking about joining a gym and maybe volunteering or looking for a job."

"Whoa!" Kacie says. "You have been doing some thinking. I haven't said anything about this before because I didn't know if you'd be up to it, but one of the companies I work with is looking for a writer on a contractual basis. You could write the assignments you wanted to write and turn down those you didn't. If you're interested, I can put in a good word for you."

"Oh, I might be. Can you text me the company's link? I'll check it out."

"Will do."

"See you tomorrow, then."

"Yes, tomorrow."

I crawl into bed with my iPad and check out the job link Kacie sends through. I haven't worked outside the home since Aiden was born. I'd planned to go back when he was six months old. Mom and Deborah offered to take turns watching him. But after he was born, I couldn't bear the thought of leaving him.

Tom came home from work and found me sobbing on the couch.

"What's wrong, Tav?"

"I don't want to leave Aiden. I don't want our moms watching him. I want to."

Tom sat down beside me and opened his arms. "Come here."

I fell into his embrace, and he held me tightly. "We'll make it work."

"But. But. But."

He kissed the top of my head. "I'll find a way."

I turned so that we were face-to-face. "Are you sure you're not mad."

"No, why would I be mad?"

"Because we were counting on my income to help pay the bills."

"We have good savings. We'll be fine."

Freya

"Mom, Emma wants me to go back to school."

"What do you want?"

"I'm torn. I want to be at school with Emma and get to graduate together. But I also know that going back will be painful."

"Principal Jones called me," Mom says. "He talked to your teachers, and they agreed to work with you for the remainder of the year."

I stare at the father and daughter across the street. He's teaching her how to ride her bike without training wheels. She falls, and he helps her up, and she tries again and again.

"I'm going to school."

"Are you sure?"

"Yes. I can't give up."

"On what?" Mom asks.

"On me."

"Well, okay then. That's settled."

"Who's that man across the street? I haven't seen him before."

Mom looks. "Roger. I passed him on my walk the other day. He and his granddaughter moved into Ruppert's place."

"His granddaughter?"

"Yes. He's raising her. She lost her parents in a plane crash."

"And his wife?"

"Roger said she died a few years ago from cancer. Seems like a nice man."

"He must be if he's raising his granddaughter." *Dad should've taken some lessons from him!*

I get out of Emma's car and throw my backpack over my shoulder. I feel as though a basketball is lodged in my throat, and I try to swallow.

Emma walks around the car and takes my hand. "You can do this."

I remember the last time I stood in this parking lot. It was the day of the accident.

"Remember what Lena said?" Emma asks. "Your family and friends are glad you didn't die."

We walk through the front door and into a sea of people. I blink and widen my eyes, trying to keep the tears from coming. My vision becomes blurry, and I feel Emma's hand tighten around mine. I hear my name and people telling me they're glad to see me. I try to smile, but smiling makes me feel guilty. *I shouldn't be happy. I don't deserve to be happy.*

I follow Emma to my locker. Nate's locker is down another hallway, and I'm grateful that none of my classes are in that same hall. I wonder if his parents cleaned out his locker.

"See what I did?" Nate opened his locker door. There are photos of me plastered all over the backside of the door.

I laughed. "You have more pictures in your locker of me than I have of you."

He leaned in and kissed me. "That's because I love you so much!"

I open my locker and stare at the photo of Nate and me on the back of the door. It's a selfie I snapped of us making funny faces. I smile slightly. Nate could be so goofy. He'd suck in his cheeks until his lips formed a figure eight and cross his eyes. He called it the cross-eyed fish.

"Everything okay?" Emma asks.

"Can we stop by the cemetery after school?"

"I thought you wanted to go to see Nate's parents."

"I do, but can we stop there first?"

"Sure."

I make it through chemistry class with the help of my lab partner Tony and survive discussing the *Iliad* in English before heading to study hall. On the way, I pass a group of boys gathered in a corner. *Nate would be furious if you looked at them. Eyes straight ahead.* And then suddenly, it hits me that Nate won't care because Nate's DEAD!

Emma waits for me outside the cafeteria, and we sit down at the table we used to sit at before Nate came into the picture. When Nate and I became a couple, he'd insisted I sit with him. I realize my life could be divided between Before Nate (BN) and After Nate (AN).

Soon, other friends join us.

"Did you see Mr. Lauer's face?" Emma asks.

I shake my head.

"I totally did," Becky says. "I don't think I've ever seen him without a beard. He looks younger."

"You look different," Emma tells Becky.

Becky blinks. "I borrowed my mom's magnetic eyelashes. They were a bitch to put on."

I want to tell Becky that it looks like spiders are sitting on her eyelids, but I tell her they look nice instead.

"How do you like my nails?" Rachel flashes her tips.

"Love the sparkles," Becky says. "I need to get mine done."

I look at my hands and squeeze my fingers shut. Rachel notices.

"You should get that polish for nail biters," Rachel says. "It worked for my aunt. It might work for you."

Nails. Summer jobs. College plans. I don't believe there is a topic we don't discuss. Everything seems so normal, except it's not. *Not anymore. Nate's dead, people. Don't you understand? He's dead and never coming back!*

I don't expect everyone to feel the way I do, but everyone seems to have moved on as if nothing happened.

Emma stops at the grocery store so I can buy a bouquet to put on Nate's grave.

"It might be cheaper to buy fake ones," she says.

I look at the fake flowers, but they look fake, and I don't want these flowers to look fake, even if they are. I don't know why it's important to me, but it is.

As I lay the bouquet on the grave, I see Lena walking toward us.

"How are you feeling today?" she asks me.

"Okay. I've been thinking about what you said."

Lena smiles. "I'm glad. You're young. You have your whole life ahead of you. I've seen people sink in guilt and never find their way out."

I begin to cry. "It's so hard."

"We don't always have control of the events that happen in our lives, but we can choose how we react to those events," Lena says. "You can either turn a tragedy into a triumph or let it defeat you. I'm hoping you choose to keep moving forward, however difficult it is."

I watch as Lena heads down the hill. "Is that her?"

"Who?"

"The woman..." My voice cracks, and I struggle to finish the sentence. "Who lost her son and husband?"

"I'm not sure," Emma says. "But it looks like Lena is stopping to talk to her. We can ask Lena the next time we see her."

As we leave the cemetery, I glance back. Lena is still talking to the woman, and I wonder if it *is* the one who lost her family, if she hates me as much as I hate myself.

I'm jarred back to the present by Emma's question. "Are you sure you want to do this?"

I nod. "The last time I saw Nate's parents was at a picnic at their house."

"Burger or hot dog?" Nate's dad asked.

Before I could answer, Nate did. "She'll take a burger with no bun."

I mashed my lips together, wondering if I should correct Nate, and ask for a burger in a bun. No, it wasn't worth getting into an argument. He had me on a low-carb diet and didn't like when I ate bread.

While Nate and the rest of his family enjoyed juicy burgers with melted cheese on a thick roll, I cut my burger into small pieces on my plate.

Tavi

I see Lena walk down the hill toward me. "I was wondering if I'd see you today."

"I'm always here," Lena laughs.

"I'm thinking that maybe I shouldn't come every day," I tell her. "What did you do when your son died?"

"Much like you, I visited his grave nearly every day. I was really sad at first, but over time, my visits grew less frequent. It became a peaceful ritual that comforted me and helped keep his memory alive."

"Is it bad if I don't want to come every day?"

Lena smiles. "Everyone's grief journey is different. You need to do what's right for you. If coming every day is too much, try coming every other day or once a week. There is no right or wrong, and no one is judging you."

"I'm struggling with what to do with his belongings. The toys and clothes are such painful reminders of the enormous loss and void in my life."

"Again, Tavi, that's an individual decision. There is no correct length of time to decide what to do with Aiden's things. I've known some parents whose child's possessions caused too much grief, and they stored them or gave them away. For me, seeing Todd's things helped me grieve. But my husband felt differently."

"What did you do?"

"We compromised. We kept some things and gave others away. In time, the box of items we'd kept became cherished mementos. Each year, on Todd's birthday, we'd open the box and hold the items. We'd hold his favorite blanket and talk about how we had to bribe him to let us wash it. We'd hold his favorite toy car and picture him sprawled out on the floor, lining up his toy cars in a straight line. We cried, but there was also laughter."

"Laughter?"

"Yes, you will laugh one day. And you will experience happiness again."

"I can't imagine being happy ever again."

"I couldn't either, and at first I felt guilty about it. I wore my pain like a heavy coat for so long that I wasn't sure I'd know how to live without it. But it got easier over time. I realized that I grieved because I loved, and I was so thankful I had that chance to love. I also learned we don't move on with grief, but forward with it."

I enjoyed talking to Lena. I could tell she was sincere. I wondered how many other people she had helped during her daily walks in the cemetery. I wonder if people come into your life because you need them to. Maybe a higher power places them in your path to help show you the way.

"Thanks for coming to chat with me," I tell Lena.

"Would you like to walk again today?"

"I can't," I explain. "I'm going shopping with a friend."

"Okay. I'll see you the next time you're here."

I watch Lena walk away before kneeling in front of the graves.

"Hey guys, it's me again. The house is so quiet, and I feel so alone. Aiden, Mommy misses you so very much. And Tom, I feel as if I'll never be able to put back the pieces of my life. I remember what you said about not selling the house if something happens to you. I'm trying to do what I know you want me to do, but it is really hard. I was thinking that I might not visit every day. Maybe every other day. I love you both."

I leave the cemetery, and as I turn onto the street, I notice an older couple walking hand in hand, and tears pour from my eyes. The thought of growing old without Tom physically hurts my heart.

"Will you still love me when I'm old and gray and wobble when I walk?" I asked Tom while putting on my pajamas.

He turned back the sheet and slid into bed. "I'm sure I'll love you more."

"Really?"

He patted the bed, beckoning me to join him. "Of course. By the time you're that old, we'll have spent a lifetime together. I'm sure we'll have children someday, and if we're lucky, they'll give us grandchildren. We'll have lived a life filled with happiness."

I snuggled next to him. "I'm sure we'll have bad times, too. Life is never perfect."

Tom kissed the top of my head. "But it's the good and the bad and the crazy and the imperfect that make life a journey and a relationship stronger."

I turned so we were face-to-face. "I love you."

He winked. "I love you, too."

I hate when a memory pops into my head without warning. I see something, or smell something, or hear something, and I'm instantly transported back in time. It's like being hit by a huge tidal wave and having the wind knocked out of you. I literally have to fight to breathe, and it's scary when it happens.

By the time I pull into Kacie's driveway, I've had a good five-minute cry. I text Kacie that I've arrived, and seconds later, I see her coming out the back door.

"Are you sure you're up for shopping?" Kacie asks.

I nod. "On my way from the cemetery, I saw an older couple walking hand in hand, and it reminded me that the future I thought I'd have is gone."

Kacie listens as I spill my thoughts, letting the words tumble over one another until the sentences form a tangled mess.

"I wish there was more I could do," she says.

I find a parking place under a light pole near the entrance to the store. "Listening and being here is what I need most."

I look at underwear on a rack while Kacie tries on bras. I walk back to the dressing room. "Find any you like?"

"I think so, but I'm only getting one. I plan to nurse the baby and will need to buy nursing bras."

Kacie and I pay for our items and head toward the food court. "Remember when this was the place to be on a Friday night?" she says.

"I remember."

"Now don't spend it all in one place," Dad told me. "And don't tell your mother how much I gave you."

I stuffed the twenty in my purse and kissed him on the cheek.

"I'll pick you up at nine," Dad said. "Right here." He pointed to the sign on the pole. "Row C, right outside the main entrance."

"I know, I know, Dad. It's the same place you pick us up every week."

Kacie and I shopped for the first hour and then headed to the food court to see who was there.

"Don't look now," Kacie said. "But Robby is at eleven o'clock. And he's with Jason. We should go over."

I casually glanced in that direction.

"Remember the flirting tips we read?" Kacie said. "Eye contact is important. And try sitting next to Jason and, during the course of the conversation, subtly bump his leg with yours."

We walked over to Robby and Jason and spent the rest of the night making eye contact, complimenting them and scoring a double date.

Kacie and I split a sub and sit near the pole in the center.

"Are you sure I can't convince you to come to Diana's party?" Kacie asks.

I shake my head. "I've been really tired. I'm going to go home and finish the series I started binge-watching last week."

"I thought you wanted to stop at the pet store?" Kacie says.

"I thought more about it. I'm not ready yet."

"You're probably right. A puppy is a lot of work."

I watch two girls, who look to be about fourteen, sit a few tables over. They stare at their cell phones and laugh. I nod in their direction. "They look so young."

"I'm sure we did, too, back in the day."

"I got the insurance money," I blurt out.

Kacie purses her lips. "How did it make you feel?"

"Mad. I haven't opened the envelope yet. It just feels wrong. It's a lot of money."

"But that money is for you," Kacie says. "It's to pay your mortgage and other expenses. It's to protect and help you."

I take a sip of water. "I know. That's one thing Tom was always very good at—taking care of Aiden and me."

Kacie and I walk to our cars. We're in Row C, right outside the main entrance.

I stop at the drugstore on the way home, and forty minutes later I'm staring at the numbers written on a check made out to me. My hands shake, and I feel tears welling up from deep down inside before exploding like steam from a tea kettle.

I'd give anything to have Tom and Aiden back. No amount of money can compensate for their loss. I think back to the conversation I had with Mom during dinner.

"Miriam asked me during bridge if you are going to file a wrongful death lawsuit. She said she knows a good attorney."

I jabbed my fork into a fry. "Miriam should mind her own business."

"Well, are you?"

I balled my hands into fists under the table. "No, I'm not."

"But why?"

"It's none of your business."

"But you could, and you'd get money."

"No amount of money can bring Tom and Aiden back. The teen made a mistake and died because of it. Thank God his passenger did not."

"That boy wasn't paying attention," Mom said. "You should be compensated for your loss."

"How many times have you driven and become distracted?"

"None," Mom said.

"Come on, Mom. You never reached to get something out of your purse and swerved a little, or maybe even went over the line?"

"That's not the same thing and you know it. I never ran a stop sign."

"Never?"

"Never."

"Well, I can't say the same thing. I ran a stop sign once when I was driving home from college. I wasn't reaching for anything. I simply didn't see it until it was too late. Fortunately for me, there were no other cars."

I tuck the envelope into my purse, planning to go to the bank the next day. Ten minutes later, I open the pregnancy test I bought at the drugstore.

Freya

Emma follows me up the porch steps, and I ring the bell.

Nate's mom, Catherine, opens the door. Her face is blotchy, and when she sees me, she bursts into tears and hugs me so hard I cough. I didn't expect such a warm embrace, and I let loose a torrent of tears.

"Please, please come in. I've been so worried about you."

Worried about me? But I killed your son!

We sit on the couch, both of us crying, as Emma retrieves tissues from her purse and hands them to us.

"Catherine, I don't know what to say or where to begin. I wish I'd died instead of Nate."

"Oh, Freya, don't say that. Rick and I are so happy you're okay."

My lips tremble. "You're not mad?"

"Mad? Oh no, sweetie. We could never be mad at you. It's not your fault."

"But Nate and I were fighting."

She pushes the hair away from my eyes. "It. Wasn't. Your. Fault."

"But if we wouldn't have been fighting..." I heave and lower my head.

She lifts my chin and, through teary eyes, she repeats herself.

I didn't hear Rick enter the room. "That's right, Freya. You're not to blame."

Rick's face is blotchy, too, and he sits down across from us. Together, we swim through a river of memories, and I'm reminded of all the good times we had. Family picnics and trips to amusement parks. The time we had a major food fight, and all of us ended up covered in cake. We laugh through the tears, and I begin to see that it's not a betrayal of Nate but rather a tribute.

Maybe Lena was right. I need to let go of the guilt so I can move forward and make something of the gift I've been given—a second chance at life.

I'm exhausted by the time Emma and I leave. "Thanks for taking me," I say as we pull away.

Mom is in the house when I get there. She waits for me to speak, but the only thing I can do is cry. A couple of hours later, I wake up to find my head on her lap and her arm around me. She fell asleep on the couch, too, and when I sit up, she opens her eyes.

"Thanks, Mom, for always being here."

She hugs me. "I'll always be here for you."

For as long as I can remember, it's been just Mom and me. Raised in foster homes, Mom met Dad when she was a senior in high school. Six months after they graduated, Mom had me.

They did what was expected and married, but I don't think they ever really loved each other. My dad's parents were in the picture for a while, but after my parents divorced, they drifted away.

I pulled the picture I had drawn out of my backpack and handed it to Mom. Across the top was written "My fanmalee" in red crayon.

I had drawn five stick figures and put a black X through three of them. I pointed to the tallest one. "That's you." Then I pointed to the smallest one. "And that's me."

Mom smiled. "You draw very well, but who are they, sweetie?" She pointed to the stick figures I had put an X through.

I point to each one and say, "Daddy. Grandma, Grandpa. They're no longer a part of our family. They left."

"Are you hungry?" Mom asks.

"A little."

"How about we go to Best Burgers?" Mom jiggles her key ring. "Would you like to drive?"

"No." I say it so forcefully and loudly that Mom jerks back. "Sorry. I'm just not ready yet." And the truth is, I don't know if I'll ever be."

Growing up, Mom and I always went to Best Burgers on Friday nights. It was the only time we ate out. Most of the time, she paid with dollar bills, but on at least one occasion, she paid with quarters she earned from her waitress job.

Five-year-old me looked at the pile of coins spread out on the tan carpet.

"We're rich."

Mom held up a paper penny wrapper. "Do you want to help?"

I eagerly nodded.

"You can separate the coins into piles." She held up a penny. "Put all the coins that look like this one here." She placed the penny on the floor in front of me before creating piles for the nickels, dimes and quarters.

"You're a good coin sorter," Mom said. "Maybe someday you'll be a banker."

"Is a banker rich?" I asked. "I need to make lots of money so I can live in a big house with a swimming pool and have two dogs and a cat. And maybe a giraffe."

"How much money do you think that will cost?"

"Umm." I rolled my eyes. "Ten dollars!"

"I met this woman at the cemetery," I tell Mom at dinner. "She was walking and stopped to talk."

"Was she just out for a walk or there to visit someone?"

"I think she was just out for a walk. She said I should see my survival as a gift, and to live each day with purpose."

"Sounds like a wise woman. She's right, you know." Mom bites into her burger, and the pickle slips out.

I jab a French fry into the ketchup puddle on my plate. "I've been thinking that maybe being an accountant isn't for me."

Mom's eyes widen, but she's in the middle of chewing, so I wait for her response. "Wow, I didn't expect that, but okay. What do you think you'd like to do?"

"I've been thinking about helping kids."

"A teacher?" Mom asks.

"More like a counselor. Or therapist. Maybe I could use my story to help others."

Mom listens as I explain all the whys behind my decision. "Well, Freya. It sounds as if you've given this a lot of thought. And it's a little surprising, considering you were never fond of seeing *your* therapist."

Mom's right about that. I hated going to Dr. Caan's, but after Mom caught me pulling out my eyebrows, eyelashes and hair, she made me.

"What's this?" Mom picked up the small pile of hairs on the desk next to where I was working.

"Uh, nothing."

"Look at me, Freya."

I turned around, trying to cover up the bald spot on the top of my head that I'd been hiding with hats and scarves.

"How long have you been pulling out your hair?"

I shrugged.

Mom pointed to my eye. "Have you been pulling out your eyelashes and brows, too?"

"Uh, maybe. A little."

Later that week, I was in Dr. Caan's office explaining why I felt the urge to pull out my hair.

"It's like an itch that you just have to scratch or it will drive you crazy. After I pull out the hair, I feel relief. But the itch returns again and again, especially when I'm stressed out."

Dr. Caan opened her desk drawer and pulled out a red ball. "Every time you feel the urge to pull out a hair, I want you to squeeze this stress ball. With practice, you'll get better at resisting the urge to pull."

I took the ball and squeezed it. Then I went to the restroom and pulled out a hair!

The next day, Mom drops me off at the cemetery. "Are you sure you don't want me to come along?"

"No, go run your errand. I'll be fine."

I walk through the ornate iron cemetery gates and pass a row of tiny old graves with lumps on top that look a little like lambs. I stop and kneel before one, tracing the name with my fingertips. *Margaret Emmeline. Born Nov. 18, 1881. Died Nov. 20, 1886.* She died before she ever had a chance to live.

As I approach Nate's grave, I see Lena heading toward me from the opposite direction.

"I wondered if I'd see you today," she says.

"How often do you walk?"

"As much as I need to," she says.

Lena's answer surprises me. She's definitely not overweight, but maybe she exercises to stay that way.

"Would you like to walk with me?" she asks.

I glance at my watch. "I can go for a short walk."

We traipse down the hill toward the other grave. The woman I saw the other day is there. I slow my pace, and Lena slows hers so that we continue to walk side by side. My heart beats faster, and I feel as if I'm going to throw up. If this woman is who I think she is, does Lena know that I killed her husband and son?

The other lady waves as we approach. She's beautiful. She has long blonde hair that's pulled to one side and hangs in a bouncy ponytail. "Hi, Lena."

I hope that Lena just returns the hello and keeps walking, but she stops.

"Hi, Tavi. How are you today?"

I stare at the grass and wish I could sink below the surface and disappear.

"I'm better," Tavi says. "Who's your friend?"

"Tavi, this is Freya. Freya, this is Tavi."

I look up and smile. "Nice to meet you."

"Same here. Are you Lena's granddaughter?"

I shake my head. *I'm the girl who killed your husband and son. I'm the reason you're here, mourning the two lost loves of your life.*

"I met Freya the same way I met you," Lena explains. "Like you, she's suffering."

Tavi looks at me. "So you lost a loved one?"

My voice cracks. "My boyfriend."

"Oh, I'm so sorry." Tavi glances at the graves beside her. "I lost my husband and son."

Because of me. I stare at my feet. I feel sick in my stomach. *Does Lena know we're connected? Should I tell Tavi who I am? I can't take it any longer.* "I killed them."

Tavi's hand flies to her heart. "What?"

"I'm the girl who survived."

Tavi's eyes widen, and her mouth opens. She looks at Lena, who doesn't look surprised, and then back at me. "I'm... I'm glad you survived."

I freeze, unsure if my dry mouth is going to let me speak. I feel the tears building. "You are? I thought you'd hate me. And I wouldn't blame you if you did. I hate myself."

Tavi reaches out and touches my arm. "I don't blame you."

"But Nate and I were fighting and..."

Tavi faces me, and places both hands on my shoulders, and looks me in the eyes. "I. Don't. Blame. You."

"But…"

"Don't," Tavi says. "You're alive, Freya. You have your whole life ahead of you. Don't waste it."

I heave and begin to sob uncontrollably. Tavi joins in the outpouring of grief, and as we hug, I feel as though a huge weight is lifted off my shoulders.

"Forgiveness is a powerful thing," Lena says.

I don't want to let go of Tavi, but my cell phone rings, and I know it's Mom. "My ride's here to pick me up."

"Do you want my number?" Tavi asks. "In case you ever want to talk."

As I walk away from Tavi and Lena, I feel as if I have been given the greatest gift of all.

Tavi

I call Kacie as soon as I get home from the cemetery. "You are not going to believe who I met today."

"What's his name? That gorgeous actor?"

"No, not Jack Allen. I met the girl who survived the crash."

"What?"

"The girl who was in the car that hit Tom and Aiden. She was at the cemetery with Lena."

"With Lena?"

"Yes."

"So Lena knows her?"

"No, Lena met her like she met me. At the cemetery. Her boyfriend is buried up the hill from Tom and Aiden."

"What the..."

"I know, it's crazy."

"Were you okay? I mean. What did you say?"

"I told her that the accident wasn't her fault. The poor girl looked like she was going to vomit. I felt so badly for her."

I don't hear Mom come in the back door. "Who do you feel bad for?"

I turn around. "Mom's here. I'll call you later."

Mom pulls out a kitchen chair and sits down. "Who was that?"

"Kacie."

"Who looked like they were going to vomit?"

I tell Mom about meeting Freya.

"Connie told me at the hair salon that the girl in the accident almost didn't make it. Her mom is a friend of one of Connie's friends."

"Well, thank God she did make it."

"You shouldn't feel so sorry for her," Mom says. "After all, she was in the car that rammed into Tom and Aiden's."

I throw the dish towel I've been holding down on the counter. "Why do you always have to assign blame, Mom?"

"Well, I'm just saying..."

"I know what you're implying. All my life, you've had to blame everything bad on someone or something. Usually, it was me. I'm not going to be like you. I'm not going to blame someone just to make myself feel better."

"I failed the real estate exam because of you."

My chin wobbled. "But I wasn't with you."

"You weren't at the exam, but whenever I tried to study for it at home, you were loud, and I couldn't concentrate."

I clutched my doll to my chest. "But most of the time, when you were studying, you made me go to my room."

"And you can go there now."

"Why is it that every time I visit, you have to start a fight?" Mom says.

"You know what, Mom. Just go. I'm really not in the mood to be with you right now."

Mom stands, grabs her purse and heads toward the door. "Soon you won't have to worry about that." A second later, the door slams shut.

I head upstairs to shower. I promised Kacie I'd meet her after work. I have something I've been wanting to tell her in person.

"I'll have water with a lemon," Kacie tells the waiter.

"Me, too," I say.

Kacie narrows her eyes. "No wine? I've never seen you pass up wine at Anthony's. This has to be a first."

I shrug. "Just being cautious, like you."

Kacie puts her hand on her stomach. "I have a reason to be cautious, but you..." She stops. "Are you feeling okay?"

I smile. "Other than being really tired, I'm feeling fine." I decide to string Kacie along for as long as I can, savoring every minute of her curiosity.

The waiter returns with our water, and Kacie picks up her glass and takes a sip.

"I'm not surprised you're tired. You had so much to deal with."

"Yes, but it's more than that." I touch my belly, and Kacie's eyes pop.

"You're not..."

"Yes, I am." I throw my arms up, and Kacie slips out of her chair, rushes around and hugs me.

"I'm so happy for you. How do you feel emotionally?"

"Happy, sad, scared. To be honest, I've been all over the place emotionally. Happy that I'm pregnant. Worried that I'll lose the baby. Sad that the baby will never know Aiden or Tom. Guilty that I get another chance to be a parent and Tom doesn't. Afraid that I won't love this baby as much as I loved Aiden. Scared like hell of doing this all on my own."

"Oh, Tavi. You're not on your own. Did you tell anyone else?"

"No. I'm going to wait a bit. I'm afraid. I keep checking my panties for blood. My obsession has become so bad that before I leave the house, I plan a bathroom break at wherever I'm going to check. I want to make sure everything's okay, you know?"

"I completely understand your fear. But you didn't have any problems with Aiden. Keep thinking positive thoughts."

"Tom and I had been trying for months. I must've been pregnant at the time of the accident."

Kacie tears up. "I'm so happy for you. And I'm sure your mom will be over the moon."

I hold up my hand. "I'm not ready to share this baby with Mom."

"But of course she'll want to be a part of your baby's life."

I sigh. "I know, but I'm not ready for her to be a part of it yet. You know how she was when I was pregnant with Aiden."

"Have you chosen a name yet?" Emma asked during the surprise baby shower she hosted.

"Aiden. I've always loved that name."

"What?" My mother sounded surprised. "I thought his name would be Henry, after your father. It's been a family tradition of passing down names generation after generation."

"That's usually on the father's side," Emma said. "Besides, just because something has always been a certain way doesn't mean it has to remain like that. I love the name Aiden."

I smiled. "Thanks, Em. I do, too. And so does Tom."

"Well, at least I'll be the first to see him," Mom said.

I didn't want to get into a fight with Mom on what was supposed to be a happy occasion. Instead, I made a mental note to confront her about her attitude.

Kacie puts her hand on her stomach. "I can't believe I ate that entire plate of chicken parmesan."

I wipe my mouth with my napkin. "I ate most of mine, too. Guess we were hungry."

"Wish that saying about eating for two wasn't just a myth, because then we'd have an excuse."

We laugh.

"I remember the doctor scolding me because I gained so much weight with Aiden. She told me I could eat 350 to 450 extra calories in my second and third trimesters, but I think I ate double that. I'm going to do better this time. Getting the weight off wasn't as easy as I thought it would be."

"I don't know what you're talking about. You looked fabulous during your pregnancy, and it seemed like you were back to a size six in no time."

"It might've seemed that way, but it took a lot of work!"

"Don't look now, but Julia Hatsboro just walked in with Jack Martin."

I drop my napkin and sneak a glance. "She hasn't aged a day. Still all legs with shiny brown hair that looks like silk. It's not fair that some people get all the good genes."

Kacie agrees. "And he's as hot as ever. Remember the time in high school when they were making out in the janitor's closet and she fell on a wet mop, and her ass was wet and Robby McManus teased her about pissing herself? I can't believe they reconnected after all these years. Don't look now, but they're headed this way."

"Hi girls," Julia says. "Jack, remember Kacie and Tavi."

Jack smiles. "Sorry to hear about your loss, Tavi."

"Loss? What loss?" Julia stammers.

She always was clueless, I think. My eyes fill with tears, and Kacie comes to the rescue and explains.

Julia's hand flies to her heart. "I'm so sorry. I hadn't heard."

Seconds later, Jack whisks her away, leaving me dabbing my wet eyes. "Will it ever get easier?"

Kacie reaches across the table and touches my hand.

The next day, Mom stops and finds me in Aiden's room.

"What are you doing?" she yells.

"What's it looking like I'm doing? Packing up Aiden's things."

Mom walks over to the box I've been filling. "But why?"

I sigh. "Because it's time."

"Who says?"

"I say, Mom. It's time for me to do this. I need to do this."

"But what about me?"

"What about you?"

"I'm his grandmother. Don't I have a say?"

"No. No, you don't."

Mom huffs and pulls Aiden's stuffed bear out of the box. "Can I at least have this? I gave it to him, after all."

"Sure, take it. What are you doing here anyway?"

"Can't I stop to see my daughter?"

"You can, but you rarely do. I'm just surprised to see you." I feel guilty for being short with Mom. "How about a cup of tea?"

▯ Splice ▯

Freya

"So, you want to study psychology instead of accounting in college," says Mrs. Godfrey, my high school counselor.

"Yes, since the...." I swallow the lump that feels like a cantaloupe in my throat. "Since the accident, I've been rethinking everything."

Mrs. Godfrey smiles as her doughy hands cut the air like a samurai sword as she explains that most students change their majors at least once. "It's something like eighty percent, so you're definitely not alone."

Her fingers dance across her laptop. "I'm going to send you a bunch of resources to check out. Do you have any other questions?"

"Not right now. Thanks for your help, though."

Emma's waiting for me when I leave Mrs. Godfrey's office. "Are you ready?"

I touch my head. "Let's do it."

Twenty minutes later, we arrive at the Shear Shenanigans hair salon. "I can't wait to see you," Emma says. "You've wanted to do this for so long."

I sit in the stylist's chair, and she drapes what looks like an oversized bib around my neck and snaps it shut. "Do you have a photo of what you're thinking?"

I pick up my cell phone and show her some images of styles I saved.

Sherry points to my phone. "I love the short, swoopy bob with blunt ends."

"I think that's my favorite, too."

"Do you want the ends to hit at the jaw or mid-neck?"

I look into the large mirror in front of me, trying to visualize what it would look like both ways. "At the jaw."

As long strands of hair fall to the floor, I imagine what Nate would say. *You disobeyed me—again. You know you need to ask me these things.*

"What do you think?" Sherry asks.

I stare into the mirror, and I barely recognize myself. Tears explode from my eyes.

"Oh, no! You don't like it." Sherry grabs a box of tissues from the counter and hands it to me.

"I love it."

Sherry gives me a hand mirror. "For a second, you had me worried." She swirls the chair around, and I use the mirror to see the back.

"It's just what I needed. Thanks."

Emma's eyes pop when I walk into the waiting area. "You look fabulous."

"Sure?"

"Absolutely!"

I touch my head. "It feels so different. Much lighter."

Emma holds up her phone. "Photo?"

I pose while she snaps a few, and then we pose together for a selfie.

"Anywhere else you want to go?"

I look at my watch. "No. I told Mom I'd be home in time to put dinner in."

I set the oven temperature to 350 degrees and slide the hamburger casserole onto the rack. The dish, made with hamburger, noodles and cream of mushroom soup, had been a staple in our house growing up.

I groaned. "Hamburger casserole again!"

"Sorry, sweetie. But it goes far."

Yeah, I know. When you make it, we have it every day for a week!

"How about making steak sometime?"

Mom opened the oven door and removed the casserole. "That doesn't go as far, and it costs three times as much. We need to get the most out of every meal. We eat what we can afford, which is hamburger and chicken and lots of pasta."

I set the table and filled the water glasses. "I bet Dad is having steak," I muttered.

"What did you say?"

"Nothing."

"You said something about your father."

"It was nothing." I slid into my seat and listened to Mom lecture me for the next half hour on the importance of counting my blessings.

I'm finishing my homework when Mom walks in. "Let me see. Let me see."

I stand and twirl around.

"Oh, Freya! I love it. You look beautiful. Why didn't you send me photos?"

"I wanted to see your reaction in person."

During dinner, I tell Mom about my meeting with Mrs. Godfrey. "She was really helpful."

"I can't believe my baby girl will graduate in two weeks. Are you ready for finals?"

"I think so. The only one I'm concerned about is chemistry, but my lab partner is helping me during study hall."

"Have you called Tavi yet?"

"I've been working up the nerve. I know she gave me her phone number, but I worry that she was just being nice."

Mom takes a sip of water. "From what you told me, she seemed very sincere. But I understand if you're not ready."

I jab a pea with my fork. "Maybe I'll call her tonight."

After Mom and I finish dinner, I head to my room and flop on my bed next to my opened chemistry book. I tap the contact button on my phone and find Tavi's number. I stare at it and debate the pros and cons of calling her. There are more pros than cons, so before I can change my mind, I call her.

"Hello."

"Is Tavi there?"

"This is Tavi. May I help you?"

"It's Freya. Freya from the cemetery." *You know, the Freya who killed your husband and son.*

"Oh, yes, Freya. I'm so glad you called."

"You are?"

"Yes, I felt badly we didn't have more time to chat."

I smile. "I'd like to talk to you sometime again. I mean, if you want to."

"Sure. What works for you?"

"Most nights. But I'd have to find a ride. I haven't driven since... since that day." I gulp.

"Do you want me to come to your house?"

"I could see if my best friend Emma or Mom could bring me to yours."

"It's up to you, but coming to your house isn't a problem for me."

"Okay, if you're sure."

I return to studying and then go downstairs to tell Mom about Tavi's visit.

Mom looks up from reading her book and says, "Are you sure you don't want to wait until I get home? I could pick up dinner for the three of us."

"That's okay, Mom. I want to talk to her alone."

"Okay, I understand," Mom says. By the way, did you see your dad sent you a postcard today? It's on the table."

"Freya, you got mail."

I ran down the steps as fast as my four-year-old feet would go. Mom handed me a postcard with Cinderella standing in front of a big castle. My mouth opened wide. "Who's it from?"

"Your dad."

"But how did Daddy get a picture of Cinderella at her castle?"

"He went to see her."

I frowned and crossed my arms. "Daddy went to see Cinderella, and he didn't take me?"

I pick up the postcard. On the front is an image of the state of Texas with cowboy boots, a long-horned steer and the words: Greetings from the Lone Star State. I turn it over and read:

I made it here. Dad.

There was no "thinking of you," or "miss you," or "hope you're doing well." I don't know why I expected more, but I did. I'm beginning to accept that he just doesn't have it in him and never will. I toss the postcard in the trash.

I text Kacie. "Can we stop at the cemetery on the way to school tomorrow?"

"Sure," Emma texts back. "R you OK?"

I text a thumbs-up. "I just want to stop."

I set my alarm and close my eyes. I can't remember when I had a good night's rest. My mind races. I think about Tavi and what I want to talk to her about. I think about my deadbeat dad, er sperm donor. I think about my upcoming exams. I remember what my therapist told me to do to quiet my mind.

I build a scene in my head. I'm on the beach. I feel the sun beat down on me, and the hot sand as it tickles my toes. I hear the thundering waves and the water lapping at the shore. Kids are jumping waves and building sandcastles.

Castles. Cinderella. Deadbeat dad! Eyes wide open—again!

The next morning, Emma picks me up twenty minutes early, and we head to the cemetery.

"Are you sure you're okay?" she asks as we pull into the cemetery.

"There's just something I wanted to tell Nate, and I know it probably sounds stupid, but I feel as though he can hear me when I'm standing next to where he's buried."

Emma waits in the car while I get out and kneel next to the grave. "Nate, I miss you every second of every day. I'm trying to move forward and focus on the great times we had, and not the bad. I'm sorry for any pain I might've caused you, and I forgive you for the pain you caused me. I'm trying to forgive myself, but I'm not totally there yet. I don't think I'll be stopping by quite as much. I can't. I hope you understand."

I look up and see Lena approaching. "I'm not used to seeing you here this time of day," she says.

"Thought I'd stop on the way to school."

"How are you?" Lena asks.

"A little better each day. I'm trying to keep in mind what you said about self-blame leading to self-harm. I'm trying to see my survival as a gift not to be wasted. In fact, I'm meeting with Tavi after school today."

Lena's mouth erupts into a huge smile. "Sounds lovely. I'll be waiting to hear all about it."

Lena continues her walk, and I get back inside the car.

I'm called to the office as soon as we get to school. Mrs. Godfrey wants to see me.

"Great news," she says as I walk into her office. "An anonymous donor has given you $20,000 to be used for college."

My hand flies to my heart, and I feel a rush of adrenaline. "You're kidding, right?"

Mrs. Godfrey hands me the check. "Someone must think a lot of you."

"I don't know anyone who has this kind of money." I examine the check. It's indeed for $20,000 and made out to me. "There's no way of knowing who sent this?"

Mrs. Godfrey shakes her head. "It came in this envelope with a note to give it to you."

I read the note. It wasn't handwriting I recognized. "I have no idea who would do this for me."

Mrs. Godfrey smiles. "You're not supposed to. That's the point. We can keep it in the office, so you don't have to carry it around all day. Pick it up before you go home."

As soon as I leave, I text Emma.

"Seriously?" she texts back.

"Yep."

"And no idea who it is?" she asks.

"None."

I decide to wait to share the news with Mom in person. I can't wait to see her reaction. I remember one Christmas we were having a particularly tough time and Mom told me there wouldn't be many presents. She was wrong.

"Freya, can you get the door?" Mom yelled.

I ran down the steps and opened the door. Omigosh! I looked around, but no one was there. "Mom! You better come see this."

I stepped onto the porch and looked at the mountain of gifts stacked so high I couldn't see over them.

I heard Mom's cry before I felt her hand on my shoulder. I turned around and buried my face in her thigh. There were presents for Mom and me, and all the fixings for Christmas dinner.

I pick up the check and meet Emma in the parking lot.

"Let me see it," she says.

"I pinched myself all day long to make sure it wasn't a dream."

"Wish I could be there when you tell your mom," Emma says. "I'm so sick of work I could throw up."

"Are they still looking for help?" I ask.

"Maybe in the deli. I'll check."

I get home just as Tavi pulls in front of the house, and we walk in together.

"Can I get you something to drink?"

Tavi holds up a bottle of water. "I'm good."

I grab a Coke, and we sit at the kitchen table. "Thanks for coming."

Tavi twists the cap off the bottle of water and takes a sip. "Of course. How have you been?"

I shrug. "I have good and bad days. There doesn't seem to be any in between, but I'm trying to follow Lena's advice and forgive myself."

Tavi smiles. "Lena gives good advice."

"Did you meet her in the cemetery, too?" I ask.

"Yes," Tavi says. She was walking and found me crying. I was really hurting and desperately needed to hear what she had to say. Lena was kind and wise and gentle, helping me move forward when all I wanted to do was die."

I smile. "Me, too. When I woke up in the hospital surrounded by beeping machines and learned what happened, I wanted to die. I thought Nate's mom and dad would hate me, but they don't. I thought you'd hate me, but you don't."

"It wasn't your fault," Tavi says. "Let me tell you a story Lena told me. It went something like this. A driver was following a truck carrying a box spring on the highway. The box spring flew off the truck and into the windshield of the car, killing the driver.

"If the driver had not forgotten her cell phone and gone back to get it, she never would've been following that truck. And if the truck driver had secured the bedspring better, it might not have fallen off."

"So you're saying when your time is up, it's up."

Tavi sighs. "Life is a crapshoot. It's full of possibilities and outcomes that we can't predict. We like to think we're in control, but we aren't. Oh, some people believe they can control the dice by gripping and tossing it a particular way. Me? I believe there's no such thing."

"So, you don't ever ask why?"

"Freya, I understand the need to understand why something happened. After the accident, I drowned in a sea of whys. But then I remembered the box spring story, and it reminded me that sometimes there are no answers. We may never know why a gunman chooses a particular day or place. And we may never understand why an illness takes a friend or family member. And we may never know why some people live and die. But we can't get lost in a sea of whys. We need to focus on living our lives to the fullest as a way of honoring those whose lives were cut short."

"You sound like Lena. She says I shouldn't waste my life. That I should practice seeing my survival as a gift. And that maybe I could use this gift to help others."

Tavi smiles. "That sounds like a good plan."

"It's what I wanted to talk to you about."

Tavi takes a sip from her water bottle. "Okay."

"I was thinking about starting a virtual support group for crash survivors and those who lost loved ones in fatal accidents. People could share their stories online and help one another. I could include resources, too. I wanted to know what you thought about the idea and if you were interested... you know, in being a part of it."

"I'm not sure how much help I can be, but I think it's a great idea. Are you thinking of a website or a Facebook group?"

"Both, maybe, eventually. Maybe start simple and see if there's a need. I've looked online for resources and there's not a lot out there. I thought it might be a way to give back and to help others who have gone through what we've gone through. I want it to be a place where people who lost loved ones get the help they need, and people like me who survived a crash get help."

I hear Mom's car and, a minute later, she walks into the house.

Tavi stands and extends her hand. "Hi, you must be Freya's mom."

"Yes. Thank you for coming. I'm so sorry about your son and husband. There are no words."

Tavi's eyes become glassy. "Thank you. You have a lovely daughter, and I'm glad she survived."

Mom puts her hand on my shoulder. "Thank you. If there's anything we can do for you, please don't hesitate to reach out."

"I think you'll be seeing more of me."

"Oh?" Mom looks at me.

"Tavi and I are working on a project together," I say. "I'll fill you in later."

Tavi

I drive to Mom's house. Normally, I would've declined her dinner invitation, but I feel guilty for being so short with her the day before. I figure she's probably ordered delivery from her favorite Italian restaurant, so I'm surprised when I find her in the kitchen cooking.

"Whatever you're making, it smells delicious."

Mom turns the knob and reduces the heat on the large kettle on the stove. "Homemade spaghetti sauce. It was your favorite growing up."

Who is this woman? I can't remember the last time she made anything for me.

"Uh, thanks, Mom. I thought we'd order delivery."

"Not tonight. I wanted to cook something special for you."

I narrow my eyes, and Mom smiles. "Can't I make my daughter's favorite meal?"

You never wanted to before. You only made it when Dad asked you to. Never because of me.

I sat on the couch next to Mommy, feeding my baby doll. The milk magically disappeared as I held the bottle to her mouth. My tummy rumbled.

"Mommy, will you make spaghetti sauce for my birthday?"

"That's too much work." She returned to reading her magazine.

I changed my doll's diaper and sang to her.

"Don't be so loud," Mommy said.

I sang softer.

"Go to your room and play. You're being too noisy."

"I haven't had your spaghetti sauce in years," I say. "I never could make it quite the way you did."

"The next time I make it, you'll have to watch," Mom says. "That way, when I'm gone, you'll know what to do."

I pull out a kitchen chair and sit down. "Mom, is everything okay? You seem different."

I realize then she's wearing the apron I made her when I was in seventh grade. *Something is definitely wrong.* "Isn't that the apron I made you?"

Mom brushes her hands over the blue gingham cotton fabric trimmed in blue rick rack. "I found it when I was going through a box of things you made me the other day."

"Oh, I didn't know you kept it."

Mom shakes her head. "Maybe there's a lot you don't know." Mom sits down across from me. "I've kept everything you ever made me, including the little pink dish you made out of modeling clay."

"All the cards I made?"

"Them, too."

I don't know why, but this revelation makes my heart physically hurt. Maybe Mom did care about me more than I thought. Maybe she did the best she could do. It hadn't been enough, but maybe it's all she was capable of.

"Tavi, there's been something I've been meaning to talk to you about."

I can tell from her broken voice and the way she's wringing her hands that it's serious.

I sit up straighter. "I have something I've been wanting to tell you, too."

"You go first," Mom says.

"No, you."

Mom inhales deeply and exhales slowly. "You know I've had some doctor appointments recently."

"I knew about your annual check-up. Have there been others?"

Mom rubs her neck. "I've actually had several. I didn't say anything because I needed time to process everything myself."

"Process everything? What's going on, Mom?"

"I have pancreatic cancer."

My jaw drops. In a choppy monologue that includes ignoring systems until the stomach pain and heartburn became too great, I learn that Mom has been dealing with this for a while.

"Why didn't you tell me sooner?" It wasn't like Mom not to share something so serious. In the past, she'd tell me if she stubbed her toe—anything to be the center of attention and get sympathy.

"What's the next step?" I ask.

"I'll have laparoscopic surgery to determine if the cancer has spread. Dr. Gupta says it involves making a few small cuts in my belly and inserting a small video camera so he can see inside my abdomen and look at the pancreas and other organs. Biopsy samples will show if it's spread."

"When?"

"Friday," Mom says.

"I'll take you."

I call Kacie on the way home and tell her about Mom.

"I'm so sorry you're dealing with all of this," Kacie says. "I know they say that God never gives you more than you can handle, but I wouldn't blame you if you felt like yelling at the Big Guy."

"Oh, believe me, I have."

I drove to the county park and parked near the large outdoor play area I'd taken Aiden to almost weekly. It was dark, and I was alone. I looked up at the sky as if I was staring into the Big Guy's face.

"Why? Am I being punished?" I screamed. "Was I a bad mother? A bad wife?"

I collapsed on the grass and sobbed uncontrollably. My entire body shook. I laid back and noticed the crescent moon.

Some say a crescent moon is a symbol of new beginnings, hope, and optimism. Others say it represents life's journey from darkness to light. A sign that a person is about to embark on a new phase and leave the old one behind.

"Did you tell your mom you're pregnant?" Kacie asks.

"I thought about it, but then she told me about the cancer, and it didn't feel like the right time." I remember Kacie has a big day tomorrow. "Don't forget to call me after your ultrasound."

"Mom says because I've been so hungry, I'm having a boy," Kacie says. "Something about extra testosterone secreted by a baby boy increases appetite."

"There are so many of those old wives' tales to predict a baby's sex. I know when I was pregnant, a colleague told me I was having a girl because my belly was high, and we both know how accurate that was."

We laugh.

"Tavi." Kacie's voice turns serious. "If I do have a boy, would you be okay with that?"

"Oh my gosh, Kacie. Why would you think otherwise?"

"Because of Aiden."

"My only wish is that your baby is healthy."

"Have you thought about having a boy?"

I nod. "Boy or girl, I'm going to love this baby to pieces. It's a gift that Tom has left me. This baby will never replace Aiden. I'm trying to balance mourning Aiden and celebrating this new baby, and it's not easy."

I get home and shower. I touch my belly. *Hello, little one. You're a very special baby, do you know that?*

I dress and slip into bed, falling asleep and dreaming a dream that has visited me more than once since learning I was pregnant.

Aiden, wearing his favorite superhero T-shirt, holds his sister, wrapped in a soft pink blanket with a tuft of blonde hair peeking out. He giggles and kisses her pudgy cherry cheek. Seconds later, I'm standing next to a crumpled car that's just been hit. Aiden and my baby girl are inside, and I can only save one of them.

I bolt up in bed and glance at the alarm clock on the nightstand. 11:11. The significance is not lost on me. Some people believe it's a magic number or a lucky time of day. Others believe it signals a spiritual presence.

I make a wish and whisper it to Tom. "We're having a baby."

Freya

"If there's anything I can help you with, let me know," Mom says after I explain the project.

"I have something else to tell you." I open my backpack, and pull out the envelope containing the check, and hand it to Mom.

Mom waves the envelope. "What's this?"

"Open it."

Seconds later, Mom shakes. "Is this for real?"

I tell her everything Mrs. Godfrey told me.

Mom looks at the numbers closer. "Who would do something like this?"

"I don't think we'll ever know. But maybe someday I'll be able to pay it forward."

Mom hands the check back to me. "It will certainly help with your college expenses. It's times like these that I'm reminded that there are good people in the world. Remember the time at the grocery store?"

"Mom, you're embarrassing me. Why didn't you check to make sure you had enough money before we bought all this stuff?"

"I must've lost a twenty," Mom said, digging in her purse at the checkout line. "I was sure I had another twenty."

The middle-aged gum-chewing cashier huffed. "Are you going to put some items back or what?"

"Excuse me," said a young mother with a toddler riding in the grocery cart behind us. "Here's a twenty."

Mom held up her hand. "Oh, no! I couldn't possibly take it."

"I insist," the young woman said. "I don't need it, and you do."

Reluctantly, Mom accepted the cash and pulled a small notebook out of her purse. "Please, give me your name and address."

I knew that Mom would pay her when she had the money.

"I still keep an extra twenty in my purse, just in case I can help someone like that young woman helped us that day."

Mom pulls out her wallet and finds the twenty tucked in a pocket between her library and grocery store rewards cards. "See, I still have it," she says.

Mom opens the refrigerator. "How about bacon and eggs for dinner? Or pancakes?"

Ever since I was little, I loved eating breakfast foods for dinner. "How about all three?"

Mom pulls out the eggs and bacon. "You make the pancakes, and I'll make the rest."

I start working on the project later that night and fall asleep in bed next to my laptop.

In the morning, Mom knocks on my door. "You up?"

"Yeah."

Mom opens my door. "Don't forget, I'll be picking you up after school to take you to your therapy appointment."

I wish the appointment had been earlier in the day. That afternoon, we had a school assembly about distracted driving and its detrimental effects on drivers and passengers. I sank down in my seat as low as I could. I know school assemblies are scheduled far in advance, but having to sit and listen to a man who lost his daughter because of texting hit too close to home.

He talked about the three types of distractions—visual, cognitive and manual—and the harm they cause. "Sentence listening takes the driver's attention off of the road and into a conversation," the presenter said. "The driver is too busy listening to what is being said and becomes distracted. This distraction prevents safe driving."

So, I guess there was a name for what happened to Nate. He was "sentence listening."

That afternoon, I tell my therapist about the school assembly. "I felt as if everyone was looking at me and judging. I should have been able to stop Nate."

"You did the best you could," Dr. Caan says. "Close your eyes, Freya. Close your eyes and imagine what Nate would say to you from a place of enlightened awareness. Would he want you to be tormented? Would he tell you that you don't deserve to be alive?"

I open my eyes.

Dr. Caan takes off her glasses and places them on the desk. "Imagine he understands you feel regret and appreciates how much you care, but he thinks being stuck in this depression and guilt isn't the solution. It's not the best way to honor him."

That night, I think a lot about what Dr. Caan had said, including her recommendation to visit the crash site, something I had refused to do. Maybe it was time.

Splice

Tavi

I'm hugging the toilet when I hear my cell phone. By the ring tone, I know it's Kacie. I stand and wipe my mouth. I've been more nauseous with this pregnancy than when I had Aiden. I call Kacie back.

"It's a boy!" she shouts. "We're having a boy."

"Congratulations! I'm so happy for you and Jack."

"Are you sure you're okay with it?"

"Yes. There will never come a second when I stop loving and thinking about Aiden. For as long as I breathe, I will grieve and ache and love him with all my heart. But that doesn't mean I won't love your son or the baby I'm carrying."

I hear Kacie cry. "That's so beautiful."

"Well, I mean it. To be honest, I'm finding strength I never knew I had. Maybe the baby has something to do with it. I need to be strong for this baby, who deserves the best I'm able to give. Though my life has been irrevocably altered forever, I'm learning to embrace this new path and pray that it leads to happiness. My life might not be the one I imagined, but that doesn't mean it won't be happy. Being Aiden's mom was the best gift I'd ever been given. Even death can't take that away."

I heard Aiden cry and eased out of bed, not wanting to wake up Tom. It was Sunday night, and he had to get up early for a meeting.

I sat on the rocker in the nursery and fed Aiden. I was amazed at the tiny human in my arms. Amazed that Tom and I had created something so beautiful. So tiny. So perfect.

I glanced at the clock. 11:11. That magical number seemed to pop up more often than it should. I closed my eyes and whispered a prayer, asking God to protect this little one. Aiden's fingers wrapped around mine, and I kissed the top of his tiny head, feeling the newborn hair tickle my lips. *My precious little boy. Mama loves you so.*

I sit with Mom in the doctor's office and wait for her test results. I thumb through a magazine and see an ad for diapers. I realize I haven't told Mom about the baby. The last two weeks have been a blur with doctor appointments and tests. No time seemed like the right time to tell her. Lucky for me, she'd forgotten I had some news I wanted to share.

Dr. Baker walks into the room and sits across from us. "The cancer is in the head of the pancreas," he explains. "I recommend removing that section, plus the first part of the small intestine, the gallbladder, part of the bile duct and nearby lymph nodes. Then I'll reconnect the remaining bile duct and pancreas to the small intestines to allow you to digest food."

"What are my chances?" Mom asks.

"I've done a lot of these procedures, and I'd say less than five percent of patients die as a direct result of surgery," Dr. Baker says. "But there are complications that you should be aware of."

We listen as he lists them: bleeding, infections, weight loss and leaking between organs that the surgeon must join. I feel a little queasy and rub my stomach.

Dr. Baker points to a graphic showing the pancreas. "It's located in a difficult spot, behind the stomach. It's a complicated procedure because it's closely connected to nearby organs. It can't be removed on its own, the way a kidney or lung can."

"But you feel confident you can do the surgery, right?" I ask.

"Yes. I've done hundreds of them. Of course, you can get a second opinion."

"Will the cancer come back?" Mom asks.

Dr. Baker sighs. "Unfortunately, the cancer might never go away completely. Up to seventy-five percent of patients undergoing surgery will have the cancer come back; sometimes it's in another part of the body. But if that were to happen, we'd use chemotherapy, radiation therapy, or other therapies to help keep the cancer under control for as long as possible."

I reach over and touch Mom's hand. "What would you do if she was your mom or wife?" I ask Dr. Baker.

"I'd tell her to have the surgery." Dr. Baker says.

Mom asks about the recovery.

"You'll spend probably about a week in the hospital after the surgery," Dr. Baker says. "Do you have help at home?"

I don't wait for Mom to answer. "She can recover at my house." I squeeze Mom's hand. "We'll fight this together."

Mom's voice quavers. "I don't want to be a bother. You have enough to deal with."

I see the puzzled look on Dr. Baker's face, but I don't feel like talking about the accident. "It's fine, Mom. It'll only be for a few weeks."

After we leave the doctor's office, I treat Mom to lunch at her favorite diner, and I wait for her to start the conversation.

"Joe Duncan had pancreatic cancer and only lasted a year," Mom says.

"Everyone is different," I say. "Dr. Baker says most patients survive the surgery and live longer than they otherwise would have. I need you to fight, Mom."

"For what? Your dad's gone. Aiden's gone."

I scrape my teeth over my upper lip, weighing whether I want to say what's on the tip of my tongue.

"I'm here, Mom."

Mom retrieves a tissue from her purse and dabs her eyes. "I didn't mean to imply that you don't matter. Tavi, I know we've never been close, and I know that it's mostly my fault. But I'm trying."

I nod. "I know, Mom. I know."

Splice

Freya

Emma and I stop at the cemetery on our way to graduation practice. The last two weeks of school have been a tornado of final exams, and I feel guilty that I haven't stopped to see Nate.

I lay the flowers I bought on Nate's grave. My heart still feels heavy, but I remember what Lena said. You cannot fast-forward through grief to get to the other side.

"Hi, Nate. Emma and I are on our way to graduation practice. I wish you were here." A shroud of sadness tightens around me, and I start to shake. I feel an arm around me, and I think it's Emma, but I turn and see it's Lena.

"He was supposed to graduate today. Instead..." I can't finish the sentence. I bury my face in Lena's shoulder and sob.

I hear the car door slam shut and, seconds later, I feel Emma rubbing my back, telling me that everything is going to be okay.

"I was doing so well," I tell Lena.

"It's okay to have bad days, sweetie," Lena says. "It reminds you how much you loved Nate, and the good days remind you that he's right there with you."

"We should be going," Emma whispers. "We need to be at the school by ten."

As Emma pulls out of the cemetery, I look in the side rearview mirror and see Lena waving goodbye.

"How have you been?" my therapist asked.

"I have good days and bad."

"Recovery from survivor guilt and trauma isn't a linear process," Dr. Caan said. "The guilt and grief of the loss come in waves, not stages."

"That's what Lena said."

"Who's Lena?"

"A woman I met at the cemetery where Nate's buried. She's been helping me."

"How so?"

I shrugged. "Just the things she says. Like not blaming myself. She's said all the things you've said."

"I see. Do you see her every time you visit Nate?"

I paused to think about the question. "Yeah, I do. She's always walking. I think she lives nearby. They built a new housing development that backs up to the side of the cemetery. She probably lives there."

Dr. Caan nodded. "Have you driven yet?"

"Every time I try to drive, I freak."

"Don't be so hard on yourself, Freya. It takes time. Like an athlete coming back after an injury, you need to ease back into it. Start out slowly by perhaps driving on your own in a parking lot, then traveling on back roads, and eventually working your way to driving on busier roads and highways."

"Are you sure you want to visit the crash site?" Emma asks after graduation practice. "Maybe you should wait until after graduation."

I open the car door. "No, let's go now."

Emma pulls out of the parking lot and heads toward the intersection. The closer we get, the faster my heart beats. I rub my sweaty palms on my jeans.

Emma glances over. "You okay?"

"Yeah, just a little nervous."

"Where do you want me to park?" Emma asks.

"Anywhere is fine."

Emma pulls over and parks along the sidewalk down the street from where a makeshift memorial has been erected. My hand trembles as I open the car door. Emma sits still and watches as I get out. Seconds later, I hear the door lock and feel a pat on my shoulder. "You didn't tell me there was a memorial set up," I say.

Emma rubs my back. "I didn't want to upset you."

I walk up to the memorial, which sits in front of a towering maple tree in a grassy area near the intersection. There are teddy bears and flowers and photos of Nate, Tavi's husband Tom and son Aiden. I kneel to get a closer look at Aiden. He's adorable, with thick, curly hair. He has Tavi's small mouth and turned-up nose. I stand and feel as though a river of regret is rising in my throat. I swallow hard to keep it from overflowing, but eventually my mental dam breaks and I throw up behind the tree.

Emma hands me a tissue, and I wipe my mouth. I recover and return to the front of the memorial site, making a mental note to come back with something special. I look out onto the road, which still contains tread marks. I bury my face in my open palms. I see Nate slam his palm against the steering wheel and hear the crunching metal. I taste blood in my mouth before I limp into the darkness.

"Let's go, Freya," Emma says.

I follow Emma back to the car. "A lot of people really cared, didn't they?"

"You mean because of all the flowers and stuff?" Emma asks.

"Yeah. It was nice to see."

After leaving the crash site, Emma pulls into the stadium parking lot at school. "I'm so glad it's not going to rain. It would suck having graduation indoors."

We join our classmates at the far end of the football field.

"You'll enter the stadium here," Mrs. Godfrey explains. "Then you'll walk around the stadium, past the bleachers on the left, to the other side where you'll enter the field and find your row and sit."

Emma leans toward me. "Are you ready for this?"

I feel lightheaded and dizzy. It's hot, and we've been standing forever.

"You don't look too good," Emma says.

I collapse on the grass.

"Give Freya space," Mrs. Godfrey says. "Move back."

Minutes later, I watch my classmates practice the processional from the shade of an overhang in front of the stadium concession stand.

Mrs. Godfrey walks over. "How are you feeling?"

"Better, thanks."

"Just follow your partner, Scott, tonight, and you'll be fine."

I nod, thinking I will look like a midget next to Scott, who is a foot taller than me.

Emma and I stop for frappes on the way home, and I tell her about the Car Crash Survivors Group I set up. "Here are the rules I came up with. Let me know what I'm missing."

I pull out my cell phone to access the site. "No promotions or spam."

"That's a good one," Emma says. "You don't want attorneys or others pushing their services all the time. I hate when people join groups, and they are only there to promote stuff."

I continue. "Respect everyone's privacy. I want to make sure that what is said in the group stays in the group."

"Another good one," Emma says.

"Be kind and courteous."

"I would add no bullying," Emma says. "And no hate speech."

"Do you really think someone would bully or talk trash about someone in the group?"

"Definitely. People can be jerks."

I'm surrounded by a sea of blue and white graduation caps and gowns at one end of the football stadium. I feel as though everyone is watching me, waiting to see if I collapse like I did during practice.

I stand beside Scott, who towers over me. An Honor Society stole wraps around his narrow neck.

Minutes later, "Pomp and Circumstance" flows from the stadium speakers, and we start walking. I scan the bleachers and look for Mom as we pass. I hear her before I see her. She's holding a posterboard that says in red marker: Congrats, Freya! You did it!

I feel my face warm, and I'm sure that I look like a radish dressed in white. I stare ahead, trying to block out her voice, which seems to be louder than everyone else's. By the time I file into my row and sit in my seat, I'm thankful for the silence.

I look up to where Nate would have sat. A white rose has been placed on the empty seat.

I can't get comfortable on the folding metal chair and start to nod somewhere between "Good evening, friends, family, faculty and fellow graduates" and "press on in the face of adversity."

I feel a tap on my arm. "You were snoring," Scott whispers.

I sit up straighter and manage to stay awake through the rest of the ceremony.

After the recessional, I see Emma bolt toward me. She hugs me so hard that I cough. "We did it!"

The crowd swells as family and friends stampede the field, and the next twenty minutes are a twister of hugs and handshakes coming from every direction.

I turn in circles, looking for Mom, and watch as she weaves through the crowd toward me.

"Freya!" Mom yells. "I'm so proud of you."

She wraps me in her arms and whispers in my ear, "I love you."

I pull back so I can see her face. "Did Dad make it?"

Mom shakes her head. "He said something came up."

Add another no-show slash to the deadbeat dad column.

I stood in my bedroom, practicing my ballet positions. Heels together, toes pointed outward, arms in front almost touching my thighs, waist curved inward.

Second position: Heels together, toes pointed outward...

Mom carried a laundry basket of clothes into my bedroom. "You're really becoming quite the ballerina!"

I flashed my five-year-old grin. "I have to do a good job for Daddy."

Mom's eyebrows jumped. "Oh, why do you say that?"

"He promised he would come to my recital."

"I see. You know that Daddy is a busy man, and sometimes he can't come to things."

"But he promised." I stomped my foot. "And a promise is a promise."

Tavi

I sit in the waiting room, trying to read a magazine, but find myself constantly checking the status of Mom's surgery on the digital wall tracker. It says, "Procedure now in progress."

I say a silent prayer and pull out the book I brought, hoping it might take my mind off Mom for a while. I know it will be hours before she's out of surgery, so I have a long day ahead of me.

My phone vibrates. It's a text from Kacie. "Thinking of you and your mom. Call me later."

I text back, "Will do."

According to the doctor, the surgery should take about six hours. I plan to go to the hospital cafeteria and grab some lunch, but I want my jittery stomach to settle first.

I read a few chapters of the book and stuff it back in my oversized purse. Kacie binges on these billionaire romances, but I just can't get into reading them. Instead, I pull out my cell phone and click on the link Freya sent to the support group for crash survivors she's been working on.

She is off to a good start with a list of online resources. I make a mental note to suggest adding some links to blogs written by crash survivors. I find a few that are well written and helpful.

My heart aches as I read some of the blogs I find. Lives lost. Lives saved. Lives changed forever.

I read about people like me—people who lost loved ones—and question why. I read about people who have survived a terrible crash and feel guilty that they were not killed, too. I read about people clinging to the past and struggling to move forward. I see me in these people, and I'm sure Freya will see herself.

My stomach rumbles, and I glance at the clock on the wall. The cafeteria stops serving lunch in twenty minutes, so I head there for a bite to eat.

I'm lost in my thoughts, recalling Dr. Baker's words: *Typically, it takes as long as two to six months to fully get back to a normal quality of life.* I wonder if I can put up with Mom for that long, and immediately feel guilty for thinking the thought. Her recent actions indicate she's trying to bridge the gap between us, so I need to try, too.

I wonder if I should've told her about the pregnancy. Especially after her comment about having nothing to live for. But I'm not ready to let anyone know besides Kacie. I want to wait until I've passed the first trimester.

Oh my God! I pulled back the sheet and saw blood. *The baby. I can't lose the baby!*

I called my OB-GYN and was reassured that sometimes it's normal to bleed, and not to panic. She said that if it persisted over the next few weeks, I should make an appointment.

A week later, I woke up to a lot of blood, and I just knew something wasn't right.

I glanced over at Tom, who was still sleeping. "Tom, wake up. Wake up! Something's not right."

When we arrived at the doctor's office, I was taken right back for an ultrasound. When the tech came in, she turned the monitor away from me.

"You see the baby, right?" I said. "The baby's there, right? You can see her."

Tom squeezed my hand. I didn't know the sex of the baby, but in my heart, I felt as if I was carrying a girl.

"I see the baby," the tech said. "I'll get you back to the doctor."

"Everything's going to be alright," Tom said. "Just think positive thoughts."

When Dr. Russo walked into the exam room, I could tell by her sullen look that it wasn't going to be good news.

"I'm sorry, Tavi. There's no heartbeat."

I felt as if I were being crushed by a ton of cement and sobbed as Tom held me. Our baby girl was dead.

"Tavi, is that you?"

The familiar voice startles me, and I turn to see Mrs. Stock, my favorite elementary school teacher. She sits at the table across from me. "What are you doing here?"

I explain about Mom. "I got your sympathy card."

Mrs. Stock reaches for my hand and squeezes it. "I've would've come to the service, but I was visiting my daughter in Florida at the time."

"That's okay. I understand. Are you here for someone?"

"My husband. He has a ruptured disk that's pressing on the nerve. Poor man has been in so much pain. I'm thankful they are finally doing surgery. Please tell your mother I will keep her in my prayers."

"I will."

Mrs. Stock smiles. "I remember your mom well. She was always so concerned about you."

"Really?" *Are we talking about the same person here?*

"Oh my, yes! She wanted to make sure you were adjusting to your new school and making friends. I told her she had nothing to worry about. You met Kacie, and the two of you became fast friends. I could tell your mother loved you so much."

"But I don't want to go to a new school!" I crossed my arms and refused to get in the car. "Why did Daddy have to take a new job, anyway?"

Mom crouched so she was eye level with me and brushed a strand of hair off my forehead. "Tavi, please give this new school a try. You're a big first-grader now, and I'm sure you'll make a lot of friends. How about you go to school without any fuss, and we'll do something special afterward to celebrate your first day?"

My arms dropped. "Promise?"

"Yes, sweetie. I promise."

I hadn't thought about the first day at my new school and Mom taking me for ice cream afterward for a long time. Maybe there were some good memories of Mom growing up that had become buried in a heap of resentment.

"Thank you for sharing that story," I tell Mrs. Stock. "I never knew that."

She finishes chewing a bite of chicken salad. "Well, you were one loved child. Every parent-teacher conference, she wouldn't stop talking about you. It was Tavi this and Tavi that. I wish all my students had mothers like yours."

Are you talking about my mom? She might've put up a good act, but she sure didn't like me much. Or at least she never showed it.

I glance at my watch. "Speaking of which, I'd better head back to the waiting room. She should soon be out of surgery."

I glance at the wall tracker and see Mom isn't done yet. I think about what Mrs. Stock said and wonder when I stopped loving Mom and started resenting her, and vice versa. Was it so gradual that I hadn't noticed, like a beach that erodes over time only to be left with a thin strip of sand? Could I have done more to stop it? *And why didn't Mom?*

Freya

Mom and I head to Emma's house for a graduation party. It's really Emma's party, but her parents are gracious enough to include me since it's only Mom and me.

"Follow me."

Emma leads me to her bedroom and hands me a small gift.

"But I don't have anything for you."

Emma bounces her head from side to side like she does when she is excited. "Well, it's really for *both* of us. Just open it."

I peel back the gold foil wrap and open the square box about the size of my palm. "It's beautiful!"

"I figured since we'll be going to different schools, we need something to keep each other close."

I pull out two necklaces. Each one contains half of a heart charm with some letters on it. When the two halves are put together, they form a whole heart with the words "Best Friends."

"This is the best gift ever!" I give Emma one of the necklaces, and we put them on and hug.

"I wondered where you two went," Emma's mom says. "Everyone is waiting for you to cut the cake."

The sheet cake is decorated with flowers in our class colors, blue and white. I'm touched that Emma's parents have included my name on the cake, which reads "Congratulations, Emma and Freya!"

"I know it's not a birthday cake," Emma's mom says as she pokes candles into the top, "but let's put candles on it, anyway."

"Happy birthday to you! Happy birthday to you. Happy birthday, dear Freya. Happy birthday to you." Nate shouted so loudly that I was sure all the neighbors heard him.

"I made it myself," he said. "Well, Mom helped a little."

I stared at the chocolate cake with chocolate icing with "I Love Freya" on top. "It's beautiful, Nate."

"Just like you."

"Ah, isn't that sweet." Mom walked into the kitchen.

"Hi, Mrs. Miller. I hope you don't mind I made Freya a cake."

"Oh, not at all."

"Want some?" Nate offered.

"Later. Do you want to stay for dinner, Nate? We have plenty."

I smile at the sweet memory that pops into my mind. Nate wasn't all bad. There was a lot of good in him at first. But somehow along the way, he slid into a jealous dark side that I never seemed to be able to stand up to. He was the one guy in my life who didn't abandon me, who loved me, and wasn't going to leave me. And that had been enough until it became too much.

Emma and I blow out the candles.

"Everyone eat up!" Emma's mom shouts. "I don't want any leftovers!"

"That was quite a party," Mom says on the way home. "It was so nice of Emma and her parents to invite us."

I touch the necklace Emma gave me. "I wish we weren't going to schools so far away."

"I know, sweetie. But you'll see each other during college breaks."

I know Mom's right, but my life won't be the same without Emma by my side, just like it won't be the same without Nate.

Later in my room, I reach for the bear holding a heart that Nate gave me for Valentine's Day the first year we were dating. I squeeze it tightly and remember every detail of graduation. Mom holding her sign and shouting. My name being announced as Principal Jones handed me my diploma. And the empty chair with the rose where Nate would've sat.

Tomorrow, I'll visit him and tell him all about it.

Tavi

I doze off and feel a tap on my shoulder that startles me. "Oh, Dr. Baker." I sit up straighter.

"The surgery went as expected. There were no surprises. Your mom is in recovery."

"When can I see her?"

"She'll be transferred to the intensive care unit, and we'll share her room number as soon as we know it."

I call Kacie to update her on Mom.

"Sounds like everything's going according to plan," Kacie says. "Let me know if there's anything I can do."

I sit in Mom's room, watching her sleep. She looks so frail, so old. A nasogastric tube is taped to her nose. Dr. Baker said they should be able to remove it the next day. The nurse comes in to check her vitals.

"I'm going to leave," I say. "She needs her rest."

On the way home, I stop at the grocery store to buy some chips. It's not normally something I keep on hand, but I've been craving them. I had the same craving with my first two pregnancies.

Freya

In the morning, I find Mom weeding in the garden. "Mom, can I borrow the car to go to the cemetery?"

Mom brushes the loose soil off her knees and walks over. "I know you've been doing well driving in parking lots, but are you sure you're ready to tackle roads?"

"I'm ready to try. If I get down the street and I get too weirded out, I'll pull over."

I follow Mom into the house, and she hands me the keys. "Just be careful. And if you get somewhere and you don't want to keep driving, call me, and I'll get Roger to bring me to you."

"Roger?"

"The man who moved in across the street. You know, the one who's raising his granddaughter."

"Oh, I had no idea you two were such good friends."

"We're more like acquaintances. We've just talked a few times, but he said that if I ever needed anything to let him know."

I take the keys, grab the bag and head to the car, but as soon as I get behind the wheel, my anxiety spins out of control. My chest hurts. I wipe my sweaty palms on my jeans and try to take deeper breaths. *You can do this, Freya. You need to get your confidence back.*

I turn the car on and take a deep breath. I don't turn to look at the house, but I'm sure Mom is staring out the window. I drive away, nervous but determined.

When I pull into the cemetery and park, I let out a huge sigh. I grab the garbage bag I brought from home in case there are dead flowers to clear from Nate's grave. I feel a bit guilty about not bringing fresh ones, but driving to the cemetery was tough enough without throwing in a stop along the way.

"Hi, Nate. It's me. I miss you. Everyone missed you at graduation." My chin wobbles, and I recount the evening out loud.

I pick up the dead flowers and stuff them in the bag.

"I wondered if I'd see you today."

My hand flies to my chest.

"Sorry, I didn't mean to scare you, but I couldn't wait to hear about your graduation." She looks around. "Are you here alone?"

"Yes, I finally got up the nerve to drive."

Lena smiles. "That's a huge step, Freya. I'm happy for you."

"Hopefully my therapist will be, too." I give Lena the graduation highlights. "It felt like the whole ceremony was in slow motion."

"Seeing Nate's empty chair must've been hard," she says.

"It was. I was going to take the rose that was on his chair and give it to his parents, but when I went to get it, it was gone."

"Maybe his parents were there," Lena says.

"Maybe, but I didn't see them if they were."

"Sometimes, people don't want to be seen. They prefer to stay in the background and be a part of the event, but not directly involved. It might've been their way of coping."

We talk some more before I leave to head home, praying that the ride back goes as smoothly as the ride to the cemetery, but as soon as I pull out of the gate, I hear a screech and then a crashing noise.

My heart pounds and I start to panic. I look to the left and see two cars. The drivers get out of their vehicles. *They're okay. They're okay.* It looks like a fender bender, and within minutes I hear sirens. I take a deep breath, trying to think happy thoughts. I weigh whether I should call Mom for help but decide to try to make it home by myself.

Tavi

I get up early because I want to be with Mom when Dr. Baker does his morning rounds. It's been a week since her surgery, and I'm hoping I can soon bring her home.

Mom had some post-op leaking at the incision site, so Dr. Baker had to insert a drain, but she seems to be getting stronger every day.

I walk into her room, and Dr. Baker is already there. "So, how's our patient?" I ask.

"She's doing well. Her incision looks great. It's been a week, and I think she's doing well enough to go home tomorrow."

"That's great news."

"Are you sure you don't mind?" Mom asks.

"Mom, we've been over this time and again. You're coming home with me."

"Now remember," Dr. Baker says. "It'll take two to six months to get back to a normal quality of life. But ultimately, you should be able to do anything that you could do before."

"When will I see you next?" Mom asks.

"Make an appointment for two weeks. I'll take out the staples in your incision then. Don't worry if you feel tightness or a tugging sensation along your incision. This is normal. Some gentle stretching can help. But if the incision becomes red or puffy, or if you have any drainage, contact my office right away."

The next day, I manage to get Mom settled in my bedroom, which I gave up because the master bathroom shower is big enough to fit a chair in. Mom complained in the hospital that it was tough standing long enough to shower properly. She also found it nearly impossible to lean back into the water to rinse her hair because her abs hurt.

"You thought of everything," Mom says, transitioning from the walker she brought home to the bed. "I'm exhausted. I'm going to rest a bit, if you don't mind."

"I always have to stay home and take care of her!" Mom shouted.

I heard my parents arguing while recuperating in bed from an intestinal virus that had wiped out most of my fifth-grade class.

"What would you have me do?" Dad lashed back. "Cancel my surgeries?"

"Your patients are always more important than me!"

"You knew when you married me that I was a doctor and would need to work a lot. You understood that."

"Well, you were the one who wanted a baby!"

While Mom sleeps, I remove the small rugs from the first floor so they aren't an obstacle for her walker. It was on my list of things to do before bringing her home, but I'd forgotten.

Mom didn't eat much, but I stocked up on ice cream, squeezable yogurt, protein drinks and other items her care team had suggested.

I take down the calendar hanging on the office wall and note the days the home care nurse and physical therapists will visit Mom. I know she's anxious to return to her own house, but I need to make sure she can get around and take care of herself first.

I yawn. It's time for my afternoon nap, so I stumble to the sofa. I set the alarm on my cell phone for three o'clock. An hour's nap will be good.

Freya

"Oh my gosh! Freya! You look as white as snow!"

I hug Mom tightly, and she reciprocates. "What happened, sweetie?"

I tell her about the fender bender. "I thought I was going to die. I couldn't breathe. It was so scary."

"But you didn't die, and you made it home all on your own. That's huge!"

Later that day, I see my therapist and tell her about the accident.

"Your reaction is normal, Freya," Dr. Caan says. "As we discussed, exposure therapy—confronting the things that make you think of the car accident—helps you to manage the symptoms of posttraumatic stress disorder."

"I wish I could just flip a switch and have my life go back to normal."

Dr. Caan nods. "Recovery from PTSD is gradual and ongoing. You have a great support network. Lean on those who love you when you need to. They want to help."

Emma is waiting for me when I finish my appointment. "How did it go?"

"Okay, I guess. Seeing Dr. Caan always helps."

Emma flashes a closed-mouth smile. She understands. She always has.

We leave and head to the mall. Emma wants to buy a new laptop with the money she received for graduation.

When we get to the store, our friend Kenny is waiting for us. He knows everything about computers and agreed to help Emma.

Kenny points to a laptop. "Best deal here."

Emma looks over the computer. "It's a little more than I wanted to spend."

I listen as Kenny makes a case for why the computer is worth every cent and why trying to save a few bucks on such an important purchase won't be good in the long term.

"This baby has tons of storage and will last you through college and beyond."

"Will the other one last me through college and beyond?"

"Well, yes," Kenny says. "But this one's the best."

Emma pauses. "Will I run out of storage if I buy the cheaper one?"

"Probably not. But I'd buy this one."

"If I buy the more expensive model, I'll have less money for other things for college."

"But Mom, everyone will know these are the fake ones. I want the real ones." I pointed to the side of a sneaker with a white, jagged line that looked like a lightning bolt. "I want these."

Mom picks up the sneaker and looks at the price on the bottom. "I'm sorry, Freya. It's too much money. I need to buy food for us. If I buy those sneakers, we'll be eating peanut butter sandwiches for a month."

I stomped. "I don't care. Just for once, I want to be like the other kids."

We walk out of the store with Emma's new computer. She bought the cheaper laptop that served her purpose, and was still able to afford a pair of noise-canceling headphones to use with it.

Tavi

My phone alarm goes off, and I check on Mom. She's still sleeping. I sit on the chair in the corner of the room. She looks like a child, with her covers pulled up to her chin and her arms crossed over her chest.

I remember Lena's advice about taking time for self-care. "It might feel indulgent, but everyone benefits, she said."

I feel more tired than usual, but I also know the first trimester is that way. I'm trying to find the right time to tell Mom about the baby, but I don't want her to think I can't take care of her. I never thought Mom and I would ever be close, but in the last few weeks I've seen a gradual shift, one I never would've anticipated.

My phone vibrates, and I slip downstairs to talk with Kacie.

"How's it going?" she asks.

"So far, so good. She's been sleeping since I brought her home."

"Want me to come over later?"

"If you want. I'm sure Mom would be glad to see you."

"When's Kacie coming over?" Mom asked during the college Christmas break. "I want to hear all about her semester."

I sighed. "You haven't asked me about my semester."

Mom dismissed me with a hand wave and walked away.

When will she ever care about me?

I hear the bell ring that I put on the nightstand and hurry to Mom. "How was your rest?"

"Good. I can't believe I slept two hours." I stand by as Mom eases out of bed. "Is it time for my pain meds?"

"Yes, but let me make you something to eat first."

"I don't have an appetite."

"But you have to eat, Mom."

We go downstairs. "How about some applesauce and a protein drink?"

"Can I eat in the living room and sit in the recliner?"

I nod and follow closely behind as she shuffles to the chair. I set the bowl of applesauce and protein drink on the small table beside the chair. "Is there anything else you need?"

"Why don't you sit with me for a while?" Mom says.

Mom has never asked me to sit with her. Most of the time, she wanted to be left alone.

I opened the doctor's kit Santa brought and took out the play stethoscope. "Please, Mommy. Just pretend you're my patient and I'm your doctor."

"I don't have time for that. Go to your room and play with your dolls. They can be your patients."

I stuffed the stethoscope back into the black case and carried it upstairs to my bedroom. I placed my doll on a chair. "Molly, you're my favorite patient. I need to give you a shot. It won't hurt. Well, it might hurt a little, but afterward, I'll give you a sticker for being brave."

"Do you want to watch a movie?" I ask Mom.

She shakes her head and sips her protein drink.

I sit on the sofa and feel incredibly awkward about the chasm of silence that ensues. I reach for a magazine to keep from fidgeting.

"Tavi, have I been a bad mom?"

I gulp.

"Don't answer that," Mom immediately adds.

"You did the best you could."

Mom nods slightly.

I feel even more awkward and change the subject. "Kacie's coming over later."

Mom smiles. "You know, I never had a best friend."

"What about Alice?"

"She's a social climber," Mom says. "After your dad died, she stopped calling and coming around. I guess without him, I was a nobody."

I'd wondered why I hadn't seen or heard of Alice recently and feel badly that I didn't ask Mom about her. "Sounds like you're better off without her."

I tried to think of another close friend of Mom's, but couldn't come up with one.

Mom yawns. "Maybe we can watch a movie."

I have a feeling that Mom wants a distraction from our conversation as much as I do.

I turn on the TV and search for a movie to watch. The hair stands up on the back of my neck when I click on a movie about a cantankerous old man who is estranged from his daughter. There's no way I can watch that with Mom. It hits too close to home. I settle for a house flipping show, which I think Mom will enjoy. But minutes into the show, she's sleeping. I place a throw over her and head to the kitchen when Kacie walks in the door.

Kacie places her purse on the table and hugs me. "How are you holding up?"

I shrug. "So, so."

"And your mom?"

"She sleeps a lot and needs to regain some strength. I thought she might be able to lose the walker in time for her follow-up appointment in two weeks, but I'm not so sure."

Kacie pulls out her phone. "I want to show you what I found for the nursery. I can't decide between a safari theme or something more whimsical."

"They both are adorable."

"I think I'm leaning toward the safari theme. Would you be okay with that?"

I'm taken aback by Kacie's question. "Why wouldn't I be?"

"I know you had an animal theme for Aiden's nursery, and I don't want to upset you."

"Oh, Kacie." I hug her. "It won't upset me at all."

"I wasn't going to bring it up, but since we're talking about nurseries, will you change yours?"

I hadn't expected Kacie's question. "To be honest, I haven't given it any thought." I can tell my eyes are glassy. "Aiden loved the animals, but if I had known he'd be so into trains, I probably would've chosen that theme."

"Which one do you like?" I asked Tom. "The story book theme or the black and white?"

Tom took my phone. "Do you have something with animals?"

I found the Pinterest board where I'd been saving nursery ideas. "How about a forest animal theme nursery? It's simple and uses a neutral color palette. I love the white crib and the wall art prints of woodland animals."

Tom looked at the photos. "Me, too. And it doesn't seem too babyish that he will outgrow it."

I hear mom and Kaci, and I walk into the room.

"How are you feeling?" Kacie asks.

"Been better, that's for sure."

Kacie lays the crossword puzzle books she brought on the end table. "I know how much you love to do these, so I brought you a couple."

Mom wiggles forward in her chair. "Thanks. That's thoughtful of you."

For the next hour, Kacie listens intently as Mom details every step since learning she had pancreatic cancer. Of course, it's all a repeat for Kacie since I tell her everything.

Kacie glances at the clock on the fireplace mantel and stands. "I hadn't realized it was getting so late. I should go."

"So soon?" Mom asks.

Kacie hugs Mom. "I'll visit again. Hope you feel better soon."

I walk Kacie out and return to Mom, but she's dozed off again. So, I grab my laptop and google nursery themes for a boy and a girl.

I'm trying to be happy about this unexpected pregnancy, but a part of me feels guilty, as if I'm somehow betraying Aiden.

I remember the times Tom and I spent trying to get pregnant. Sex seemed like a means to an end, and it was hard to relax. Month after month, I was filled with grief, unable to conceive the child I desperately wanted until it finally happened. And then I lost her.

When Aiden came along, I was afraid to get too attached, fearing that I might lose him, too. But then I realized that being connected to my baby was worth the potential pain. He was the answer to a prayer, and he deserved the best I could give.

This pregnancy feels different for so many reasons, and I'm scared because it's my last chance to have Tom's child. I'm constantly checking for blood in my panties and strangely happy about morning sickness. I want to feel the baby move so badly, but I know I'm just not at that point. But I need the reassurance of feeling the baby move to know he or she is okay.

I close the laptop when I hear Mom stirring. "Can I get you anything?" I ask. She shakes her head and I take a deep breath. I'm ready to share my news.

Freya

"I think Kenny likes you," Emma says.

I jerk my head back. "What?"

"Kenny likes you."

I shake my head. "I don't think I'll ever go out with a guy again. Maybe I'll end up being a nun."

Emma rolls her eyes, stashes her new purchases in the trunk of her car, and we head to a nearby coffee shop, one we've never been to before.

This time, I order a vanilla Frappuccino without the whipped topping and sprinkles, just as Nate would have wanted. I'm not sure why. Maybe it's a way for me to connect with him. Weird, I know.

"My treat," I tell Emma and hand the cashier a twenty.

We sit in the corner, and I notice a sign on the wall across from us. It says: C.O.F.F.E.E. Christ offers forgiveness for everyone, everywhere.

I visibly shake, and I can tell that my emotions are building and about to crescendo into tears.

"Are you okay?" Emma asks.

I wipe my eyes and point to the sign.

Emma turns around.

"It's weird, isn't it?"

"What's weird?" Emma asks.

"That certain things come to you when you need it the most. Take Lena, for example. Meeting her has been a godsend. She's helped me so much. And that sign, appearing when I was just thinking that Lena is always reminding me of God's forgiveness."

Emma shrugs. "I'm not sure. But I do think that when something is top of mind, you start to notice it everywhere. Like I never really paid attention to the color of cars, but when I got my red car, I saw red cars everywhere!"

We finish our coffee, and my eyes linger on the sign as we leave. As we drive home, I point out all the red cars on the road.

"See, that's what I mean," Emma says. "You're thinking about red cars, so you see them."

"Do you mind if we stop by Nate's parents' house on the way home?" I dig his class ring out of the pocket in my purse. "I think they should have this."

We ring the doorbell, and Nate's mom answers the door. "Freya, come in."

I notice the rose, the one that had been placed on the chair during graduation in memory of Nate, next to a framed photo of him on the small table in the foyer. "I can't stay long." I nod to Emma's car. "Emma's waiting for me." I open my fist to reveal Nate's ring. "I thought you should have this."

Mrs. Myers's chin trembles, and she takes the ring. "Are you sure?"

I nod. I weigh whether to ask her about being at graduation but decide not to. I don't want to upset her. I nod toward Emma's car. "I should be going."

Mrs. Myers extends her arms and hugs me. "You're always welcome to visit."

"How did it go?" Emma asks when I close the car door.

"I think she was glad to have Nate's ring. She told me she was going to put it on a chain and wear it forever."

Mom isn't home yet, so I fill out a job application for a barista at the coffee shop we were just at. I had scanned the QR code at the counter when I paid for the drinks. Maybe it was yet another sign that I was meant to work there. *C.O.F.F.E.E. Christ offers forgiveness for everyone, everywhere.*

Tavi

I sit across from Mom. "There's something I've been wanting to tell you."

Mom sets the crossword puzzle book on the counter.

"I'm pregnant."

Mom's jaw drops. "With Tom's child?"

"Of course, with Tom's child."

"Sorry, I didn't mean... it's just that—"

I interrupt. "I was pregnant at the time of the accident, but just found out. With everything that was going on, I hadn't noticed that I missed my period."

Mom leans forward, and a tear drizzles down her face. "I'm so happy for you, Tavi."

I can't stop crying, and I end up as wet as a mop dipped in a bucket of water.

Mom cries, too. "I can't believe we get a second chance."

"More like a third," I say. I had never told her about the miscarriage, but I share that now.

"Oh, Tavi," she says. "Why didn't you tell me about this when it happened?"

"You and I have never been close," I say. "Truth be told, I thought you hated me most of my life."

Mom buries her face in her hands and cries. "I wish I would've been a better mother. I have so many regrets. I wish I had done a lot of things differently. I'm ashamed that I was so jealous of you and the relationship you had with your dad. I'm ashamed that it took getting cancer to make me see how badly I treated you. Will you ever be able to forgive me?"

I nod. "Lena says that forgiving ourselves and others allows us to move on. This is a new beginning for both of us."

Freya

My phone rings, and I roll over in bed and grab it from my nightstand. I sit up. "Yes, I can come in for an interview today. One is good. See you then."

I find Mom in the kitchen. "You're up early for a Saturday."

"I have an interview at the coffee shop."

"They sure didn't waste any time contacting you. Sounds promising."

I cross my fingers. "I hope."

Mom sips her coffee. "When should we leave?"

I get a mug from the cabinet. "I want to try driving again."

"Are you sure?"

I nod. "I want to do this by myself."

"Well, okay then, but I'm here if you change your mind."

I call Emma and tell her about the interview. "Great, text me afterward," she says. "I'll check my phone when I get a break."

I search my closet for the perfect outfit to wear and settle on a woven wrap dress with a V neckline and ruffled sleeves. It was one of Nate's favorites. Maybe it will bring me luck.

Mom waves goodbye as I pull away. I take a deep breath and grasp the wheel with both hands. *You've got this, Freya. One block at a time, one stretch of highway at a time.*

My palms are sweaty, but I don't dare take them off the steering wheel. When I turn into the coffee shop parking lot a wave of relief washes over me. *Thank God, thank God, thank God, I made it!*

Fifteen minutes later, I walk out with a frappe and a new job. I text Mom and Emma and head to the cemetery to tell Nate.

"Nate, I have some good news." I kneel on the ground and place the flowers I bought at the grocery store on my way to the cemetery. "I start tomorrow, and the manager said when school begins, they'll work with my class schedule."

I see Lena at a distance and wave. She approaches with a smile as big as the sun. She always seems so happy, and I wish I knew her secret.

"I see you brought new flowers," she says.

"Yeah, but I also wanted to tell Nate about my new job as a barista."

"That's great news, Freya. What coffee shop?"

"The one by the mall. Emma and I stopped there yesterday, and I saw they were looking for help."

"I know the one," Lena says. "How's the project that you and Tavi are working on going?"

"Well. The Facebook group is growing, and people are starting to share stories and resources they find helpful."

"That's wonderful. You've planted a seed. Continue to water it and watch it grow."

Tavi

Over the next two weeks, Mom gradually gains strength, and when she returns for her follow-up appointment with Dr. Baker, she walks into his office without her walker.

"You're doing great," Dr. Baker says. "You're ready to schedule chemotherapy. I'm sending you to Dr. Tan."

Three weeks after having surgery, Mom has another procedure to install a port. A week later, chemo starts. The plan is for her to have six four-week cycles. She gets an infusion on weeks one through three and takes a daily oral chemo pill. She has a week off before beginning again.

I stop by the store on my way to the cemetery to get some anti-nausea patches and protein shakes. Trying to make sure Mom eats 1,000 calories a day is challenging because she has no appetite.

"Hey, guys. I know I haven't been here for a while." I run my fingers over the grave marker. I fill them in on what has been happening, and when I turn to go back to the car, I see Lena waving in the distance. I wave and wait for her.

"I've been thinking about you," Lena says, "wondering how your mother is doing."

"She has good days and bad days," I say. "It seems like just when she starts to feel better, another round of chemo begins."

Lena nods. "I remember those days well."

I wait for her to elaborate, but when she doesn't, I let it go. "Funny how cancer changes your perspective on things," I say. "Mom and I have never been close, but cancer has opened a door I thought was forever locked."

Lena smiles. "Cancer does change your perspective on what's important. Often, we get caught up in little things that really don't matter. For example, I never let the kids eat in the living room. Then one day I did, and one of them spilled a glass of soda on the carpet. Instead of freaking out about it, I simply cleaned it up. It left a spot, but every time I looked at that spot I was reminded of the fun they had that day eating where they had never been allowed to before. We shouldn't let silly things hijack the important ones."

That night, Mom and I eat in the living room.

Splice

Freya

"I didn't know you worked here." I hear a familiar voice and turn around to see Kenny.

"I started about a month ago. How have you been?"

"Busy. I'm taking two college classes. I was anxious to get a head start."

"What can I get you?"

"Regular coffee. Black."

I get Kenny's coffee and hand it to him. "This one's on me."

He smiles. "Maybe we can get together some time."

"Maybe."

"Well, that's better than no," he says and walks out the door.

After work, I stop to see Nate. I feel guilty that when Kenny suggested going out, I felt a little tingle inside. I'm scared of the tingle.

When I get out of the car, I see Lena emerge from the hedges on the left.

"Hi Freya," Lena says. "How's the new job?"

"I like it, but I think I need to stop drinking so many frappes." I pat my stomach.

Lena dismisses my remark with a wave of her hand. "Nonsense. Anything else new?"

I decide to confide in Lena about Kenny. She is always so helpful. "A guy from high school came into the shop today."

"I imagine you see a lot of old friends there."

"Yeah, but this one's different. He kind of asked me out."

"Oh," Lena says. "I see. And you're not sure if you should go out with him."

I shrug. "What will people think? Is it too soon? Not that we will be boyfriend and girlfriend, but would it be too soon to go out on a date?"

"There's no right or wrong time to consider dating again. It could be weeks, or months, or years. Listen to your heart, and don't try to satisfy someone else's idea of when you're ready."

When I get home, I hear Mom laughing, and I walk to the backyard and find her sitting with Roger, watching his granddaughter blow bubbles.

"Oh, hi," Mom says.

Roger stands, and the little girl runs over. "I'm Roger and this is my granddaughter, Baily."

I shake his hand.

"Do you want to help me make bubbles?" Baily asks.

I smile. "Sure, I can help."

I follow Baily and as I walk away, I hear Mom and Roger laughing again. I can't remember Mom ever being with a man besides my dad. I guess the time is right for her to start dating again.

Splice

A Year Later

Freya

So much has happened over the past year. I have two college semesters under my belt, and the survivors group Tavi and I started is flourishing. I'm still working at the coffee shop and dating Kenny. Emma decided to study abroad for a year, but we Facetime daily. Mom and Roger are getting married, and we are moving in with him and Baily. I think of Nate often, but with the help of my therapist, Lena, family and friends, I'm living again.

As I look in my rearview mirror at that awful afternoon of the crash, I see fear that has turned into courage and weakness that has turned into strength, and I am grateful to be alive.

A Year Later

Tavi

I look at the baby girl in my arms, and I am amazed at how perfect she is. Born at 11:11 on a Saturday night, her name is Hope. I am beyond blessed to have her in my life. Lena was right; it is possible to love my new baby and also grieve the child I lost. I think Aiden would be happy his sister sleeps in his old room, now a palace of pink everything.

Mom visits often, and our relationship has grown in love and respect. Tom's mom, who moved to Florida after Tom died, visits as much as she can.

Forgiveness really is a powerful thing. Kacie and I have weekly playdates, and sometimes we even manage a girls' night out. Thanks to Hope, life is good, and I am well.

Epilogue

Tavi pushes Hope in the baby carriage, and Freya carries three red roses. They place one on Nate's grave and the other two on Tom's and Aiden's graves. A crowd of people surrounds my grave. They have gathered to remember me on the tenth anniversary of my passing from ovarian cancer. As Tavi and Freya walk by, they stop to see whose headstone everyone has gathered around.

Lena Stark
Loving mother and wife
1955-2020

....

May the God of hope fill you with all joy and peace in believing, so that by the power of the Holy Spirit you may abound in hope.
Romans 15:13

Chapter 1
Gina

The bastard was dead.

I stared at the newspaper clipping Mom had mailed me. I'd read his obituary online, but seeing it on paper in front of me made it more real. Kind of like watching the Wicked Witch of the West melt in the "Wizard of Oz" – all the evil you loathe becoming a puddle of nothing.

Richard M. Smith, 61, was ushered into Heaven on Saturday, February 11, 2012, surrounded by his family at his home.

I'm pretty sure he went to Hell.

He was a loving husband, devoted father and dedicated coach.

He was the biggest asshole on this side of the Mason-Dixon Line. Maybe on the whole East Coast. Oh, what the hell, let's just say the entire country. You get the point, he was an A-S-S-H-O-L-E, and I hated him more than I've ever hated anyone in my life.

Mostly because he ruined it.

I grabbed my high school yearbook off the shelf in my office. Mom brought it on her last visit. She was cleaning out the basement, and it was among the things she didn't want to throw away or take to Goodwill.

I opened the book and read the message I've read so many times I know it by heart.

Gina,

To the best and sweetest girl any guy could have. You're super in every way and you mean everything to me, and don't ever forget that! You know I don't like to write because I can't express myself as well as if I would tell you but I'll try anyways. I love you very much and want our relationship to last! You're just a super girl, you care about me very much and I appreciate it because it makes me feel great inside, and I feel very lucky to have a girl as great as you. If I had to sum everything up about you in one word it would have to be amazing! It probably sounds dumb but that's the way it is. I just want to let you know that I do love you and will do anything for you that you want me to.

Love, Mike

I remember his black hair and curls. His five o'clock shadow in the middle of the day. The way his smile took up most of his olive face and the way his dark eyes danced when I walked into the room. I remember the first time he told me he loved me, and the first time we made love. Why is it that you never forget your first love? Maybe it's because it's the first person you gave your heart to, completely. The first time you were afraid to breathe for fear the moment would pass and you would miss some of the seconds. Life is seldom what we think it will be. Especially when you're seventeen and the biggest concern you have is whether someone has the same prom dress.

I ran into Mike once at the pizza shop in town. It was the day after Christmas, and I was home visiting my parents. I saw him as soon as I opened the glass door and the bell jingled. He stood at the counter, holding a baby bundled in blue. The sight washed over me like a damn wave that you never see coming until it's too late and you're face down eating sand. And just as you try to spit out the sand and stand up, you get knocked over again by the damn hot pizza smell that transports you back in time. Back to the night you ate pizza in the corner booth that still has your names carved in the wood. The night you got drunk on the six-pack you took from your dad's stash in the garage. The night you made out in the woods and fell asleep naked intertwined like pretzels under a crescent moon.

He turned and saw me and then came the smile. His white teeth seemed even whiter, his smile broader. There was small talk and more small talk. About his marriage and baby and move across town.

What happened? What happened to all the plans we had? All the nights we spent lying under the stars sharing our dreams. The kind of house we'd live in, how many kids we'd have. What their names would be. What happened to us?

Life. That's what happened. One day comes after another and another and pretty soon you realize that yesterday was pretty damn long ago and that everything you had hoped for is never going to happen. You can't control it any more than you can control that big wave from getting stronger before it nails you. All you can do is prepare and hope that when it hits, you'll survive.

And hope that the secret you've kept all of these years doesn't drown you.

Facebook
www.facebook.com/AuthorBuffyAndrews

Goodreads
www.goodreads.com/author/show/
7113753.Buffy_Andrews

Website
www.authorbuffyandrews.com

Amazon
www.amazon.com/Buffy-
Andrews/e/B00EO7F1IG

About the Author

Buffy Andrews is USA TODAY and Amazon best-selling author. She has showcased her versatile writing skills across a spectrum of genres and target audiences. Whether delving into women's fiction, young adult narratives, middle-grade stories, or picture books, she has demonstrated mastery in each realm. A two-time Pulitzer judge, she was a journalist for nearly thirty years before starting Andrews Creative Concepts, a digital marketing agency. She lives in southcentral Pennsylvania with her husband, Tom.